Reviews for

By <u>Angel Wing Buyer</u> on January 30, 2012

I must confess that I don't read a lot of romance or genre fiction, so I was pleasantly surprised by the spiritual depth and emotional maturity of Her Last Chance by Danielle Zwissler. Without spoiling the plot, there's a whole lot more going in the lives of Kat and Warren than meets the eye, and the author very cleverly layers this story so that the full complexity isn't revealed until the end (when readers realize that there has been a higher purpose to the twists and turns of their lives all along!). What makes this story the most remarkable, though, is that Her Last Chance delivers all of the passion and heat you expect in a modern romance--all the while building their spiritual connection as well (without ever delving into saccharine religiosity. Can somebody say "Amen?") The effect is a fulfilling book on many levels--and it leaves me wondering why it hasn't been made into a Hallmark or Lifetime movie yet? Seriously, at one point, when the brave but deeply traumatized Warren (who's been reading Kat's advice column without her knowledge) says to her "I fell in love with your words," I became a puddle! (Pass the Kleenex, please!) I can't tell you why that scene pierces the heart without giving crucial things away, but let me say this: if you're looking for a well-developed romance that reminds you of all that is good and true in this world, filled with flawed but delightfully real people who aren't about to let a good thing go, this is the book for you. Did I mention it's a series? Enjoy! :)

By <u>Proud_Army_Wife</u> on February 18, 2011

Romance novels are not my typical read but Her Last Chance is different, the story is heartfelt and attainable. The way Kat and Warren come together could be happening to other couples right now!! I could not put this book down, I was drawn into the Daniel's family and their crazy fun loving way of taking care of each other. Bill seems like an overbearing nosy dad but he really just wants what is best for his daughters, and gets a laugh in while doing it. :)

By <u>Phyllis L. Seibert</u> on September 18, 2011

There are many parts of this book that I absolutely love. I am especially taken with Katherine and Warren's "first date." I love the fact the author writes about how our lives are preplanned and how even though we are not sure what we want, there is always someone at work nudging us along. I became completely entrenched in the desperation, want, and refusal that Warren's and Katherine's relationship has. I found myself laughing, crying, and cheering for this couple.

The surprise ending will blow you away. This book was not a disappointment. I could not put it down. Even though, it is a smaller book, it is full of emotion and detail.

By <u>poolgirl9</u> on May 25, 2011

Katherine thinks she has it all and doesn't need anyone until Warren comes along. She is funny and love dumb. Warren is smart and funny and patience with not only Kat but with her dad Bill. Bill is funny and always up to something. Pick it up and enjoy.

It makes you realize that last chance is always worth the risk. You will love these two. Enjoy it.

By <u>Amazon Customer</u> on October 3, 2011

Read it in one sitting. The flow was spectacular, the characters were beautifully flawed, and the sweet romance between Kat and Warren was perfect :) Great job, Danielle! :)

By <u>S. Bish</u> on February 9, 2011

I love the characters in this book. This was my first Kindle purchase and I could not stop reading. The story sucks you into their world because it is so down to earth and believable. I can't wait to read more from Danielle!

HER LAST CHANCE

THE DANIELS DYNASTY: KAT & WARREN

DANIELLE LEE ZWISSLER

Firefly & Wisp Books

www.fireflyandwisp.com
ISBN: 978-0-9827062-0-6
Library of Congress Control Number: 2010927420
2015 Print Edition

First Firefly & Wisp Publishing Printing 2010

Dedicated to:

Earl, the barriers finally crumbled. I will love you forever.

Acknowledgements:

To my beautiful children: Ariana and Logan Zwissler. I love you more than anything in this entire world. To Krista Bowden: a friend from high school that took the time to read about Warren and Kat's story, and to Wesley and Rise' Haver, my parents. Thanks for college... I think it may have helped.

Danielle Lee Zwissler
Her Last Chance

Firefly & Wisp Books
A Blush Special Edition
Romance

Thank you, God, for everything.

The Race

"Quit, give up, you're beaten"
They shout at you and plead
"There's just too much against you
This time you can't succeed".

And as I start to hang my head
In front of failures face
My downward fall is broken by
The memory of a race

And hope refills my weakened will
As I recall that scene
Or just the thought of that short race
Rejuvenates my being

Children's race, young boys
Young men, how I remember well
Excitement sure, but also fear
It wasn't hard to tell

They all lined up so full of hope
Each thought to win that race
Or tie for first, or if not that
At least take second place

The fathers watched from off the side
Each cheering for his son
And each boy hoped to show his dad
That he could be the one

The whistle blew and off they went
Young hearts and hopes afire
To win and be the hero there
Was each young boy's desire

And one boy in particular
Whose dad was in the crowd

Was running near the lead and thought
"My dad will be so proud"

But as they speeded down the field
Across a shallow dip
The little boy who thought to win
Lost his step and slipped

Trying hard to catch himself
With hands flew out to brace
And amid the laughter of the crowd
He fell flat on his face

But as he fell his dad stood up
And showed his anxious face
Which to the boy so clearly said
"Get up and win the race"

He quickly rose, no damage done
Behind a bit that's all
And ran with all his night and mind
To make up for the fall

So anxious to restore himself
To catch up and to win
His mind went faster than his legs
He slipped and fell again

He wished then that he had quit before
With only one disgrace
"I'm hopeless as a runner now
I shouldn't try to race"

But in the laughing crowd he searched
And found his father's face
That steady look which said again
"Get up and win the race"

So up he jumped to try again
Ten yards behind the last
If I'm going to gain those yards he though

I've got to move real fast

Exerting everything he had
He regained eight or ten
But trying hard to catch the lead
He slipped and fell again

Defeat, he lay there silently
A tear dropped from his eye
There's no sense running anymore
Three strikes, I'm out, why try?

The will to rise had disappeared
All hope had fled away
So far behind so error prone
A loser all the way

"I've lost, so what," he thought
I'll live with my disgrace
But then he thought about his dad
Whom soon he'd have to face

"Get up" the echo sounded low "Get up" and take your place
You were not meant for failure here
"Get up," and win the race

With borrowed will "Get up" it said
"You haven't lost at all"
For winning is no more than this
To rise each time you fall

So up he rose to run once more
And with a new commit
He resolved, that win or lose
At least he shouldn't quit

So far behind the others now
The most he'd ever been
Still he'd give it all he had
And run as though to win

Three times he'd fallen, stumbling
Three times he'd rose again
Too far behind to hope to win
He still ran to the end

They cheered the winning runner
As he crossed the line first place
Head high and proud and happy
No falling, no disgrace

But when the fallen youngster
Crossed the line, last place
The crowd gave him the greater cheer
For finishing the race

And even though he came in last
With head bent low, unproud
You would have thought he'd won the race
To listen to the crowd

And to his dad he sadly said
"I didn't do too well"
"To me you won," his father said
"You rose each time you fell"
Written by
D. H. Groberg

Preface

*L*ove could be so unexpected. She could still see him; his face was etched in her mind as the ambulance made its way through the small, residential area. Her lip trembled as she cried out his name over and over again. Her father was sitting next to her, his hand covering her own. She couldn't breathe; she couldn't speak as she closed her eyes once more.

A few minutes later, she was lifted out of the ambulance as the EMTS pushed her gurney through the double doors of the slight Connecticut hospital. She could hear everything, but opening up her eyes caused pain that she didn't want to feel. She heard her father speak once again, "It's okay, baby. We aren't mad at you, we love you. Your mother and I—we love you!" he sobbed.

Strangely, Katherine didn't care. She'd wanted to be anywhere but with him at that moment. She didn't care where she went as long as she wouldn't have to see this place ever again with its people, animals, and little children—all happy. The diseases, God-fearing idiots, drunk drivers, drug-abusers, and terrorists. *What was so great about here?* She didn't know. Obviously, the big guy upstairs would know, and if he was real, maybe she would ask him. Nothing she experienced had been that great— absolutely nothing, except for her brief life with Warren.

Warren.

Her lip trembled once more, and she felt her body shake. The monitor on the machine that she heard beeped.

One long beep.

Dead.

She was dead.

Good.

No more life, no more worries.

A blank slate.

***

She floated in a space just above her bed and continued up through the room. The light that had once been blinding was now far away and mellow. She could see black all around her. *Space? No, no stars. Is this death? This isn't half bad*, I say to myself. Then she heard it; them. Voices: her family, friends, her life. It was all falling apart, and for once, she didn't have to deal with it.

"Kat!" she heard her mother calling her. She was crying.

Katherine felt herself being tugged down. She watched. Her mother was standing next to the bed near collapse as her father put his arms around her. She fell over, and fainted. Her father had caught her mother just before she hit the ground.

She could see them now. Well, pictures of them, and they were floating around her like miniature television screens all tuned in to her life. Not just of what was happening now, but what had happened in the past. Everything that she had ever done was in front of her, screaming at her to notice.

The pictures moved past her as she watched them, she

detected that they were all of the bad things, the questionable things that she had done over the years, starting with when she was just a little girl. She looked up, remembering the time vividly.

It was her.

She sat on the floor with a pair of scissors and her brother's new coat. "I remember this," Katherine whispered. "Oh, this is the time when I took my brother's jacket and cut it." *Yes, that was funny.* Now she sees something that she hadn't seen before—her brother in the corner crying. The coat was his favorite. His other one had stains, and he was made fun of for it. Now she felt horrible. A tear slid down her cheek. It was a new feeling, as it had been years since she had cried. She was now overwhelmed.

There was more.

Every action had a positive and negative reaction. She knew that now. Not that she didn't know the concept before, but for the past few years she couldn't quite grasp much of anything—nothing since Warren died.

Warren was her boyfriend of five years, and they had been inseparable. It had practically been love at first sight, and then he was driving home one evening after work, and she had never seen him again. She didn't know if he was alive or dead, if he had run away from their life, from her. He just vanished, as if he had never been there in the first place. As if the last five years were a figment of her imagination. They never found his car. They couldn't even find a trace of a credit card.

She tried to move on and almost succeeded, until two years ago when she got the call that they found his body.

He was dumped off somewhere in the woods, disregarded as if a human life was a waste, as if he were trash.

He was murdered.

Her heart broke.

The whole tragedy came right back and crashed down on her. She was as good as dead two years ago. The fact that she had made it a whole two years was a testament of her will to live. She lost her mind, her feelings, the ability to cry, and more importantly, the will to live. Which, of course, brought her to her current status.

Now, more pictures of her life came alive. A moment with Warren...This was when he asked her to marry him. It was such a beautiful day. The sun was out, no clouds. She couldn't help but smile at the memory. They were sitting on the beach when he rolled over on the sand to her towel and had this seashell in his hand. He held it in his palm and asked her to take it. Katherine thought he was being silly, so she told him no. His eyes pleaded with her, and she laughed and playfully took it out of his hand. In his palm was an emerald-diamond ring. It was small, so she rolled her eyes and told him when he could get serious about her and get a better ring she would accept. She laughed a little, thinking that he would do the same. Looking back, she wished she wouldn't have. Now the next part came into view. More pictures of Kat's life were flashing in front of her; Warren working extra hours, him pushing an alarm clock at three in the morning. *Why?*

He threw his clothes on and pulled into this warehouse that she had never seen before and started shoveling...Fish? *He worked on the docks? When did he*

She watched some more. He looked tired as he shoveled and shoveled and continued until the clock struck seven a.m. Some guy named Charlie came up to him and pat him on the shoulder.

Warren looked and spoke, "Only five more weeks of this, and I can buy that ring!" He smiled.

"Wow, Warren...Marriage. That's great! Do you have a picture of your girl?"

"Of course," Warren said happily. He pulled his wallet out of his back pocket. "Now, don't touch the picture. It's all I have. Isn't she beautiful? I just hope she says yes."

"Ah, man, any guy who works two jobs and smiles like a fool every time he talks about his girl is sure to get a yes. What's the ring look like?"

"Well, it sparkles like her eyes. It's not huge, but I think it's her. It has one slit of an emerald in the center, and there are nine diamonds around it. It reminds me of her, my Kat. It looks like a cat's eye, and not to mention, the nine diamonds."

"Damn, that sounds great. Do you think she'll like the emerald?"

"I hope so. It's the color of her eyes. Make no mistake, it will suit her; I just hope she says yes."

Katherine started to cry. Just looking at Warren brought all of the good and bad memories back to her. "GET ME OUT OF HERE!" she said, screamed was more like it. Why didn't he tell her that he worked so hard? She would have been.... "GOD! GOD! If you exist, why don't you get me out of this hell? GET ME OUT OF...!"

"Hello, Katherine," the voice called out.

"Who's there? Who are you?!" she yelled.

"Ah...you know exactly who I am, don't you?" The voice said.

She sat down in the dark space and folded her legs under her. She searched the room for a face, but got nothing. She screamed again, "Please! Get me out of here!"

After a minute or so she could see Him. God. She started to cry. Ashamed, she covered her face. Tears came down her skin and she could feel her body start to shake. She felt sick. It was hard to breathe.

"Take a deep breath, Katherine. It's okay, I'm here."

She inhaled deeply and immediately felt better. She straightened her shoulders and stood up. He walked over toward her and held out His arms. She ran the rest of the way to Him. "I'm sorry! I am so, so sorry!"

"Do you know what you did?" God asked.

"I... What I did?"

"Yes, Katherine. What *you* did. *You* gave up on life. Do you know what you did?"

"Life gave up on me! You're God; you put me in this place."

"I also gave you free will. You have the ability to turn things around. You have control over your own destiny.

Katherine couldn't help but think that it seemed like such a God thing to say.

"Things are tough, Katherine... Ask my Son, he'll tell you. Not everyone can be bent to your will."

Is he joking? Is God making a joke? This is not funny. His Son? Damn't he's talking about Jesus in a time like this. "What are you talking about? Are you telling me that you couldn't stop Judas?"

God smiled. He stood back and paced the room and rubbed His chin with His thumb and forefinger. He was much taller than she expected, and He wasn't white either. If she were being honest with herself, it was kind of freaking her out. His voice was deep, and He looked Middle-Eastern—almost like a terrorist, or what she imagined a terrorist looked like. *Thank God He can't hear my thoughts!*

"I'm not a terrorist, Katherine," God said. "And not all Middle-Eastern people are either...you should know that." Her eyes widened. He could hear thoughts, too. She freaked out. Then tried to stop and clear her mind.

It wasn't working.

"It's hard to be here, isn't it?"

"Where is here?" Katherine asked, trying not to think about what was going on around her.

"Limbo."

"Limbo? What do you mean? This isn't heaven?" she asked.

God started to laugh, and not just a chuckle, but a big old belly laugh. "Heaven's no!" He said, laughing at His last remark. His eyes twinkled.

"What's limbo?"

"The land between the Heavens," He said, and pointed up, "and Hell." He looked down under His feet at the blackness.

"Oh," is all she could muster.

"Oh," He said as He looked into her eyes. "So, you called?"

"What? I...yes...I don't wish to see these pictures anymore. I want to go with you, where it's happy, where I can see my Warren again."

"Ah, I thought that may be what you wanted," He said, then put his hand back up to his chin and rubbed. "No."

"What do you mean *no*?"

"No. You will remain here. This is your one-way ticket to limbo. You killed yourself, Katherine. Apparently you can't remember the contract we had before you entered into the living."

"Contract? I—" She didn't remember any contract. For heaven sake, she was born into the world, and then she..."

God stood before her and pulled a long piece of parchment out of His pocket. Her name was at the top scrawled in gold: Katherine Elizabeth Daniels and it was her signature. This had to be a joke.

"No joke," God said.

"Stop doing that!" Katherine cried.

"What?"

"Stop listening to my thoughts! How did you get my signature?" she asked, and then all at once she remembered. She was there before, only it wasn't exactly here. It was in the place that they call heaven. She was a flash of light before. She signed the paper agreeing to the life that God had found for her, created for her, and she was to enter; learn to live. She was given a gift. Not everyone could go down. Angels remained up in heaven for training. She was special, God told her, and now she had ruined it. How could she have...?

"Forgotten?" God asked. "Many do. You lost your way, I'm afraid. You did just as many did to my Son, you forgot about your purpose, your will. And now I'm afraid you will remain here with the lost. Hopefully, someday you will find your way." A light surrounded him, and He started up a staircase that wasn't there before. She yelled for Him to stop.

"One more chance," she pleaded. Tears started streaming down from her eyes; she launched herself at His feet. She pulled Him back down the steps. He looked down at her sadly and wept. After his tears diminished, he held out his hand and pulled out another sheet of parchment.

Katherine breathed a sigh of relief, hoping that He was giving her what she thought it was... a second chance. "This time, I'll get it right, I promise! I want to share a life with you. Please, let me go with you! Let me see my Warren again! Please?"

"I've got a better idea, Katherine. Don't mess this one up," He said as he peered down at her. "Let's just call it *one last chance*."

"Anything, God, anything. You won't be disappointed!"

God looked up with a thoughtful expression and smiled. "I suppose not," He breathed, and then held out his gold pen once more.

Katherine felt its familiar structure in her hand. She smiled up at Him as He watched her sign the paper, and then, like a flash, He was gone, and she found herself screaming again. Only this time, the scream was not of anger or of happiness. It was one of agitation, and she could see her father. He was young, and he was smiling as he was saying something to her mother.

Something about a cord.

"She's so beautiful, Gail," her dad said.

"I have so much planned for you, baby girl. You're mommy's special little lady," her mom cooed.

Katherine couldn't help but think that she had a lot planned for herself, too, as she pulled her little hand to her mouth and sucked her thumb.

Oh, shit.

CHAPTER ONE
Thirty-Eight Years Later...

*K*atherine Daniels saw him looking at her through one of those "sideways" glances, and her heart skipped a beat nearly every time he had done it. She couldn't bring herself to acknowledge the flirtation between them; she could only turn beet red at the thought of it. Kelsey Martin was the Editor in Chief of *High Fashion Magazine*, and he certainly knew how to get women to fawn over him. Only she didn't want to be just any other woman.

The Boardroom for *High Fashion Magazine* was full. She, being the advice columnist for the magazine, was expected to turn in her latest column. Her friend, Lacy, the cosmetologist, Janice Wheeler, the owner of High Fashion Magazine's daughter and also in charge of print production, and Kelsey, the Editor in Chief, sat in the room planning the next month's layout.

"Hey, Kat, I need your column on my desk right away. I know this isn't the *New York Times*...but...we still sign your checks," Janice said, smirking.

Kelsey cleared his throat as Katherine began to speak. "I have the specs ready for you now." She shifted through a few papers then pulled out the ones she wanted and handed them across the table. Janice was in charge of large print production and ran a tight ship. She wanted the articles on her desk at least five hours sooner than the deadline—supposedly in case of "magazine emergencies". Yet everyone knew it was because she was anal retentive with a side of bitchiness. *High Fashion* was indeed not the *New York Times*. The Times was a more than reputable journalism position, one that she has strived to obtain since college. It was serious—unlike, *High Fashion*—lipstick and shoes. She wanted to give real advice. Advice that went further than "How to entice your man in bed" or "What to do on that special date."

Janice took the papers and placed them on the pile in front of her. "Thank you, now onto other business. I need to have production up at least twenty-five percent this quarter. Kelsey, get on your columnists. We need more spice, pizzazz. We need something hot like Angelina Jolie or Prada. I want the Halloween cover to be scary but posh. I want the key demographics buying this magazine tenfold over Glamour and Cosmo."

"What do you suggest I do, Janice, hire a new crew? We have the October issue already finished. Not spicy enough?"

"Please, Kelsey. I get spicier things out of my nightly glass of Vodka. See me in my office for your next assignment." Janice's eyes rolled to the back of her head before she stood, glaring at Kelsey and then to the rest of the staff.

Kelsey nodded his head in agreement, and rubbed the back of his neck his right hand. He looked stressed.

Janice looked at everyone just then and spoke, "Okay, folks...let's get to this. And, if I may add, this magazine is called, "*High Fashion*", please don't embarrass us here by wearing the latest garage sale items. Shareholders stop in here every day. They take notice to what you're wearing." Looking directly at Katherine, she smiled nastily. The others in the room glanced around. Kelsey looked down at his suit and shrugged his shoulders, Lacy glared at Janice as she stole a glance at Katherine, noticing her blue sweater. Katherine looked embarrassed.

"This is cashmere, Janice," Katherine said quietly.

"And it's very nice, dear, but you're a professional. Start dressing like one."

Embarrassed, Katherine walked out of the room and straight to her cubicle.

* * *

Katherine, red faced with humiliation, buried herself into her work once again. She hated working for Janice. She was nothing but a spoiled rich bitch. Janice Wheeler had it out for her ever since she published her first article for the *New York Times*. Rumor has it, Janice tried to freelance for a few other high profile papers and magazines, but her articles didn't cut it. The only reason why she had her job in the first place was because of her father. Her *articles* were turned down before they even hit the drawing room. It's not that Katherine was special. Freelancers were a dime a dozen. She didn't know why she was the target for Janice's hatred. All that she could think of is the newest article that she wrote and hoped that the New York Times would pick it up.

Katherine leaned over, picked up her purse, and grabbed her compact. She looked into the mirror, noting her appearance. Her brown hair fell like a blanket past her shoulders. Her green eyes looked good outlined with the black charcoal pencil she used before she left her apartment. The lipstick that she wore was still on, making her lips look nice and full. She checked her teeth to make sure nothing was in there. Seeing no evidence of the bagel with cream cheese, she shrugged, and then looked down at her sweater. There was nothing wrong with the way she dressed. Just last month the sweater that she wore was worn by Arianne Zucker, an actress on "Days of our lives." Only Katherine bought the more cost worthy of the two at Macy's. Shaking her head out of frustration, she closed the compact and placed it back in her purse. There was no reason for her to be embarrassed. She knew what jealousy did firsthand, and she wasn't going to fuel the fire anymore by paying heed to it.

Just then, her phone rang, bringing her attention away from Janice. "Hello?" Katherine said pleasantly.

"Katherine, hi, it's Tawnya Morgan, from the circulation department of the *New York Times*. I just wanted you to know we want to run your article. We'll probably run it sometime before Thanksgiving. Carrie Stevens will be off for a few weeks and we need to fill up her column spot. We'll probably run it then."

Katherine inhaled deeply and smiled. "Thank you so much for calling, Tawnya. I know I always ask this..."

"Are we looking for anyone to replace Carrie?" she interrupted, and then laughed.

"Yes," Katherine sighed.

"Actually, there is something else you should know. The freelancers that turn in their articles for this particular week are going to be considered for her replacement. I would say you have as good a chance as anyone. How many articles have you had run now?"

"Four—five when this one goes through."

"I'd say you have a great chance then. Hopefully, someday, we will actually speak face to face! Good luck, Katherine. Oh, and your check will be mailed the week after the article prints. No change in address?"

"No, everything is the same. Thanks again, Tawnya."

"No, problem. Good luck and I'll talk to you later."

Katherine hung up the phone with a smile on her face. Her day was just beginning to brighten. She glanced over to her inbox that lay on her desk. She perused through her mail to see whom she would hand out advice. When she did this, she would always look at the bigger picture. Many of her successful articles were problems. Most of them, she thought, weren't real problems, such as what kind of wine went with what kind of meat, or how to let a guy down easily, if not interested. That being said, she never gave advice about marriage, children, or in-laws. Those things she knew nothing about and didn't feel right giving untested advice. However, when she came upon this particular letter a few months ago, she couldn't let it go. This letter was the same one that Tawnya was talking about. This could be her chance for serious journalism. She couldn't wait for Janice to read it, or to see the reaction of the staff of *High Fashion*, and she definitely couldn't wait to see Kelsey's blue eyes sparkle as he devoured her words.

That night after she finished reading through her mail, she dropped another article off on Janice's large pile of papers. She closed the door and pulled her parka over her head as she pushed the elevator button.

The twenty-third floor of the New York building was by far the busiest. People pushed the button several times during the day, many bringing articles up, photographers turning in their newest snapshot, and the paparazzi flying in with the latest scandal.

As she waited for the doors to open, she daydreamed about Kelsey. The prospect of the two of them together seemed so promising. Sadly, she knew nothing of the man, other than how he took his coffee in the morning or that he always wore his blue and white paisley tie after his article went on the magazine awards listing.

Kelsey Martin was well-built with blonde hair and beautiful, blue eyes. He was tall, too, and he dressed to the nines. Katherine couldn't think of even one time where he came to work wrinkled or disheveled. He certainly was not the hag that she had been today—*blue cashmere. I mean really, how yesterday!* she thought, laughing to herself.

"Going down?" a deep voice came from behind her.

Katherine turned to look, and Kelsey was smiling at her, his finger poised over the button ready to push. She smiled nervously. "Yes, thank you."

Another smile crossed his perfect lips as he pushed the one button. "I hear your article will be in the New York Times tomorrow, Katherine."

He called her Katherine. No one ever called her by her whole name before. Yet, when he said it, it sounded so sexy. "Tomorrow? No...and how did you hear that?" Katherine asked.

"Oh, you know the newsroom. Things go around there like wildfire."

Katherine nodded in agreement. The place was a cesspool for gossip. "Oh, I actually did get a call today from them, but it won't be in for a few more weeks. Sometime before Thanksgiving, they said. I just hope they like it."

"I'm sure everyone will. You know you're a wonderful writer," he said with a grin.

Katherine blushed, "Well, thank you. I'm flattered that you think so."

Kelsey smiled even bigger as the elevator began to slow to the first floor. "Well, off we go." He gestured his hand out for her to go first. "Shall I walk you to your car?"

"Oh, thank you for offering, but it isn't necessary. I'm meeting up with my friend for drinks tonight." *Lie, lie, and lie*, she thought to herself.

"Oh, that's ok. I just...well, have a good time tonight, Kat."

Back to Kat again. "Thanks. You, too." She turned to face the curb of the outside of the building and hailed a cab. Another night at home alone, when she could have had old blue eyes walk her to her car. She didn't have a car, but he didn't have to know that. She could have just wondered around the parking garage aimlessly spending time with him. She could have made up a car theft, anything to be near him. *What was it with her that made her turn into an idiot when it came to men?* Was she doomed to write her story as a tragedy, talking her way out of one bad relationship to the next? She just needed to relax, let her guard down for once.

Her apartment building must have been one of the smallest that New York City had for rent. Her tiny studio consisted of about forty square feet with all of the amenities of a stove, refrigerator, shower and toilet. She couldn't believe how small it was for the price she was paying. She came from a small, rural town in East Connecticut. She had a huge family, and the house was one of the biggest homes that she had ever seen. So, moving into the tiny New York apartment had been an adjustment to say the least. Her mother and father couldn't understand why she wanted to live in the city. She could've paid a lot less for a much bigger place in the country, but she couldn't get past the excitement of the Big Apple. She loved the architecture, the hustle and bustle of the crowd, the great taste of a hotdog at two in the morning. She loved the noise. She loved the rush of the New York traffic; she was a New Yorker even if it said, "Connecticut" on her birth certificate. She was a true city girl.

She jangled her keys as she walked up the two flights of stairs. She pushed one in the lock, slowly opened the door, and reached for the light switch as she walked in. Her apartment, for being so small, was incredibly cozy. The dark mahogany bookcases, stocked with books, lined the outer walls. Her couch was a warm red, which invited anyone who walked in to sit down on its cushions. The walls were a rich tan that held decorated prints from famous artists like Van Gogh, Monet, and Renoir. A single afghan draped over the back of the couch, which she used from time-to-time while watching a movie late at night. She had a Murphy bed that pulled down to reveal a full size mattress with a microfiber duvet; she loved the softness of it against her skin.

Her kitchen was little to be enthused about. She had a tiny, apartment sized stove and refrigerator, and her table folded down also. But, all in all, she was happy with her place because it was her own. *And,* she didn't have to share it with her sister and five brothers.

When Katherine finally sat down in front of her flat screen television and grabbed the afghan to curl up with, the phone rang. She stood up and reached her arm around the back of the couch to one of the bookcases. Her cordless made its home there with a basketful of change and some other miscellaneous items. "Hello, Katherine speaking."

"Hi, Katherine, it's mom," came her mother's cheery voice.

"Mom, how are you doing today?"

"Well, Kat, I'm doing pretty well. *Unfortunately*, your father isn't. He has to have another surgery. The doctor heard a murmur today in your father's check-up. A few other things came up also."

"Oh, Mom, I'm so sorry. How is Dad taking this?" Kat asked as she stood up. She walked over to the small kitchenette and pulled a coffee mug off one of the pegs under the cabinets.

"Well, he's a trooper. He said this is the last one, he's sure of it. He's always positive about these things. Thank God, because I'm on the verge of a breakdown."

"It's going to be okay, Mom. Is there anything that I can do to help?" Kat scooped coffee from the Maxwell House container and filled the brewer and pushed the button.

"Well, it's funny that you should ask, Kat. I really need you to stay with your father for the next few weeks. I understand that you have an important job there, but your brothers…they're not a big help, and you, after all, are your father's favorite."

"What about Karen?" Kat asked, feeling horrible for even suggesting it.

"Your baby sister has enough problems. She has a new boyfriend."

"No need to say anymore on *that* subject," Katherine said as she laughed. Her mother did her best impression of one of Karen's last boyfriends.

"Mom, I don't know if I can get off right away. When's the surgery?" Kat asked, as she waited for her coffee to finish. She sighed, "I do have some vacation time coming, but I'm not sure if Janice will give it to me. She's been difficult lately." More like a pain in the ass, but her mom didn't need to know that.

"Everything okay?" her mother inquired.

"Yeah, just a little work jealousy. I have another article going into the New York Times," Katherine said enthusiastically.

"Oh, that's great, Kat!" she exclaimed and then paused. "You know…I wouldn't have asked you if I thought it wasn't important. See if you can get some vacation time, and come out to Connecticut to visit. I would do it again, but my boss said that if I take off for another two week stint, I will no longer be welcomed back. And, since this is our only stable income, and where our health insurance lays, I have no choice really."

"When's the surgery?" Katherine sighed.

Her mother blew out a deep breath. "I knew you would come through for us, Kat. You always do. It's on the eighteenth—ten days away. Your father will be going into Mercy General. I appreciate everything that you're doing.

You know that, don't you?"

"Yes, Mother. I'll talk to Janice in the morning, and get back to you sometime tomorrow. Don't forget to start looking out for my article in the Times...it should be sometime before Thanksgiving."

"I wouldn't miss it. I will get several copies and brag to anyone that will listen."

Kat laughed. "I know."

Bye, dear."

"Bye, Mom. Give my best to Dad."

The phone went to the dial tone. She had to take off work to care for her father. She hadn't taken a vacation in the eight years that she worked for *High Fashion*. According to payroll and Human Resources, she was owed sixteen weeks of paid vacation, not including her sick days. She hated to miss work. She had only missed three days since she started and they were bereavement days for her Grandfather's funeral. Still, she felt awful for not being there. She put the phone back on the charger and turned to sit back down on the couch. The last thoughts that went through her mind before drifting off were of Kelsey. She pictured herself all cozy and nestled up next to him on her soft bed.

***

The alarm sounded just shy of five a.m. She stretched her arms high above her head and turned to the side. Her neck was sore. She hadn't fallen asleep on the couch in a long time. She stood up, and took the short stroll to the bathroom. Her clothes thrown to the floor, she turned the knob on the shower and began to refresh herself for the new day ahead.

After about twenty minutes, she was ready and grabbing a bagel with cream cheese before making her way outside.

The New York streets were alive that Wednesday morning. Familiar faces donned the sidewalks as they hailed cabs to their prospective work places. Women pushing strollers with little babies while listening to their mp3 players rushed past with all the on-comers, as tourists were running amok with their video cameras pointing at the different sites. Katherine felt as if she were in a moving picture. She loved the rush of the New York mornings. The fast moving scenes as they unfolded around her. She loved her life, except for the one tiny detail, she didn't have much of one.

She rushed through the swiveling door, pushing it as she walked into the drab entryway. The elevator stood directly in front of her. She reached out to push the up button when she felt someone next to her.

"Going, up?"

Kelsey. She'd know his voice anywhere.

"Kelsey, yes, we seem to keep meeting this way," she said nervously. Her face flushed from the sound of his voice.

"We do. Ready to start the day?"

"Yes, and no. I have to ask for a few days off." *Why am I telling him this?*

"Really? Need a vacation?"

Yes, desperately, in some hot place with you; your arms wrapped around me...Wake up, Wake up, Wake up, Kat!

"Kat, are you okay?"

"What? Oh...sorry, no. Not a vacation, my father is

getting a surgery; I need to help my mother around the house and with him."

"Oh, I'm sorry to hear that. I hope he's going to be okay." He sounded worried for her. She couldn't believe that someone this gorgeous could also have a sweet side. She wanted to see more of it.

"Oh, that's okay. He'll be fine. I, on the other hand, am worried what Janice will think about this. She doesn't exactly promote my fan club."

Kelsey, chuckled. "Janice is just...Janice. I'm sure what she said to you yesterday was out of...jealousy." Kelsey winked at her and pushed the button to the twenty-third floor.

"Thank you," Kat said as she stepped in. "I don't want any problems. I just want to do my job, and live my life." *Stupid, stupid, stupid.*

When the door to the elevator opened on the twenty-third floor, people on the other side of the doors came in. Katherine and Kelsey exited and walked down the hallway into the newsroom.

"Wait, Kat," he said, stopping in front of her. "I was wondering if maybe... Would you like to go out to dinner with me?" He looked down nervously and when he looked back up his eyes were warm.

"Oh, I, yes, when?" she stammered.

"Since you're going away soon, how does tonight sound?"

"Oh, it sounds...wonderful, thank you." Katherine couldn't' believe her luck. She tried not to smile like an idiot.

"Great! I'll pick you up around eight then?"

"Eight, sounds fine. I live at…"

"Twenty-eight Birmingham place…"

Too late. Her eyes widened at the mention of her address. How did he know where she lived? She looked at him curiously, her face beaming into a grin.

"Sorry, I used my position to gain your address…"

"No, that's…"

"Scary, I know. I just thought about a hundred times on how I was going to ask you. I even went over there two weeks ago and buzzed, but chickened out."

She smiled a soft smile at the mention of the buzzer. She remembered a few weeks ago when she heard the buzzer, thinking it was for takeout. She buzzed them up and nothing. She thought Mike's Chicken and Eatery forgot her food. *Note to self, apologize to Mike*. She couldn't believe what she was hearing now. He'd been thinking of her, too. All of a sudden, she felt as if things were turning around for her in the love department.

"I was going to say sweet. But, scary may be a better fit," she replied. He looked at her and smiled.

"Well, eight it is."

She turned away from him on cloud nine. It was eight a.m. and she had twelve hours to go until she was alone with the man of her dreams.

Her cubicle was as tidy as it could be. Papers stacked up higher than usual, lay in her inbox. They were all letters for her prospective advice column. She couldn't imagine how busy she would be after her article went out. The phone rang, startling her from concentration. She picked up the receiver and a familiar, "hello," rang out on the other end. It was her father.

"Dad, how're you doing?"

"Well, Kitten, I'm doing a little bit better. I thought I would call to see if you're able to help your mom and me out?" He sounded enthusiastic rather than ill. She wondered if this surgery was necessary.

All she could do is feel sorry for herself. She was going to miss Kelsey, and being with her father for two weeks would be *okay,* but definitely not great.

"Well, I was just going to talk to Janice. I'll find out in a little while. Other than that, what's going on?"

"Oh, nothing really. Your mother has me on a strict diet as usual. Egg whites, toast, low fat butter, same old same old. I'll tell you, though, it's not that bad. But don't tell your mother, I enjoy getting her all riled up!" He laughed a little.

"Same old tricks? You sure make her work for it, don't you?" Kat laughed as she thought of the many times her dad teased her mom.

"Always. So, dear...any new boyfriends that I should know about?"

And there it was... she had to check her watch. Only five minutes, if that, into the conversation. A new record if you didn't count Christmas of 2003, that was after the kiss at the front door. "I'm seeing someone this evening—for a date."

"Nothing serious, though?" her father inquired.

"Not yet, but you never know, why?" Kat frowned. Her father was usually happy about her getting a date. It was all she ever heard about how she hasn't provided him with any grandchildren yet.

"Oh, you know me...just trying to see how my baby girl is doing." He sounded a little unsure of what he was to say next. "So, this will be okay then, leaving this new guy for old guy?"

"Old guy?"

"Me," her father piped in.

"Father, I hardly think that's an option. You're having a surgery; of course I'll be there for you. I've known Kelsey for a few years now, and I'm sure he'll still be here when I get back." She couldn't believe she just said that. He would be there, wouldn't he? She mentioned his name. *Shit. Stupid, stupid, stupid*.

"Kelsey, huh?"

He caught the sudden name drop. Why wouldn't he...*damn it!*

"Kelsey Martin? Editor in chief, Kelsey?"

"Yes, father, the same."

"Oh, isn't he taking advantage of his position?" her father joked. "You know you could have a sexual harassment suit against him."

"Nice, Dad. That's hardly necessary. Although, thanks for worrying. He isn't taking advantage in any way; besides, maybe I want him to."

"Lovely, dear, just lovely. Well, I'll let you go on that note. Talk to Janice, and please let your mother and I know your plans so I can make my plans with Dr. Vance."

"Will do. Love you, Dad. Give my best to mom. Bye."

She heard the phone click and she hung up the receiver. Her father still, after Thirty-eight years, was in her business. She couldn't believe how easy it was for him

36

to pry; her life was such an open book to her family because there wasn't really anything there. Having five brothers and one sister, she'd never really brought a guy home. She was always afraid for his life. When her brothers asked about her dates, she would say they were just friends so she would get away with not bringing them home to meet the family. If she had, her date would've been put through the ringer. If she really didn't like a guy that kept pestering her, she would bring him home. On the one occasion that she did, her brothers ended up liking him and became one of their best friends. Then, unfortunately she had to see the loser all of the time. Tommy Jones still to this day had a thing for her.

"Katherine, I heard that you needed to see me?" Janice's voice rang out of the entry to her cubicle. She made herself at home in one of the chairs seated next to Katherine's desk.

"Oh, who told you?" Katherine's eyes looked bewildered.

"Well, I just ran into Kelsey in the hallway." Janice looked over her shoulder, then turned and faced Katherine. "He said you had an emergency, and needed some time off." She sounded concerned and reached her hand across the desk to touch Katherine's. Katherine, thrown off by the gesture, stared down at Janice's hand until she removed it.

"Oh, yes, I'm sorry that I didn't get to tell you first. I didn't know Kelsey would say anything or I wouldn't have told him. My father is having a surgery, and I need to help him for a few weeks, to get him back into good health. Is that okay, Janice? It'll be in ten days, and then I will need at least two weeks off."

"Kat, say no more. I've checked with Human Resources, and according to them, sixteen weeks of vacation are owed to you, not to mention you only took three bereavement days...so, according to them, that's another twenty four days saved. Just let me know when to expect you back.

"Is there any way that you can still write your column away from home? Maybe you can do a story about your father in the hospital to satisfy our readership, or maybe a self-interest story about going back home? November's magazine articles are to be about being thankful and thankful about our bodies...but, thankful for your health is good enough for your advice column. Just as long as we are following a theme," Janice said energetically.

Katherine bit her tongue back from saying something snotty.

"I can still write my column for sure. You would need to either forward the mail to my parent's home or I can get a P.O. Box...what do you think?"

"I think that sounds like a great idea. You can email me your column, and I'll forward it to the printers. By the way, no hard feelings about yesterday. You look like you took my advice about your clothing." Janice smiled, and the look wasn't so innocent.

Kat felt the anger start to bubble up, then she calmed her thinking. "No hard feelings, I've had this outfit for a while now. I saw Kate Beckinsale in something similar last night on the red carpet to her premier for, "Serendipity" so I figured I was safe. I mean if Kate Beckinsale, can wear it, why not me?" Her last comment was meant sarcastically, but Janice didn't seem to get it. No wonder she never had anything of importance published. Her wit didn't seem fit for a hillbilly comedy club.

After Janice left the room, Katherine picked up the article that she responded to for the New York Times. She grinned down at her words on the page. She was very passionate when she gave advice in her column. This letter was by far the hardest that she ever dealt with. She felt for the man. She didn't know if she could take her own advice if she were in his predicament. But she did know that if she was, she would be glad to read the words. She was sure that he would feel relieved at her expert opinion, if you could call it that. If only he left a return address, or a phone number. She could've called him and suggested some extra counseling sessions, or talked with him one on one to make sure that her advice was indeed the right way to go.

Sometimes in her profession, she wished she had the time to answer everyone's questions by getting to know him or her better. Countless times she had gotten letters back from people saying that they loved her advice, took it and were happy with the outcome. On the rare occasion, she got hate mail. She hoped that this time the man could move on, and learn to love again. "Confused in Connecticut" wouldn't have to wait much longer for his response letter; it was to be printed within the next few weeks. She hoped that she would find out if she gave the right advice or if he was able to get help on his own. Either way, she felt hopelessly connected to him.

As she finished up with the rest of her work that she

had to do that evening, she couldn't believe how fast the day had gone. It was already time to go home. She had her date in a few hours and would have to find something to wear that did Kelsey justice. She couldn't imagine what that would be; she might have to stop at the store before going home. She wanted to look perfect for their first date.

CHAPTER TWO

The buzzer to her flat rang as she was putting her sling-back heels on her feet. It took her five outfit changes before she found the right thing to wear. She couldn't believe how nervous she was, but this was, after all, Kelsey Martin. The man practically had style tattooed across his forehead. He was sexy. She ran over to the intercom, and spoke clearly, "Come on up."

She didn't know what their plans were yet. She'd spent the better part of two hours cleaning her flat. She dusted the furniture, and folded her laundry. Then, after the wardrobe malfunction, she scented her apartment with her new Victoria Secret perfume. The intoxicating fragrance wafted through the flat like a summer's breeze, making her blood rush. She hoped that it had the same effect on Kelsey.

A soft knock at the door told her that he was waiting on the other side. She took one last look in her mirror, flattened her skirt and took a deep breath. When she opened the door, a fist full of red roses and a box of chocolates were waiting for her.

"You look beautiful, Katherine." He smiled a big smile. His eyes sparkled as they met hers. She could barely breathe.

"Thank you," she said, taking the flowers and chocolates. "I'll find a vase. You look incredible. I hope you didn't have trouble finding..." Suddenly she felt warm. She remembered their conversation from earlier. His previous visit when she thought he was the chicken man.

"You remembered." He chuckled nervously as his face slightly reddened. "Well, I thought we could have dinner, catch a movie and *maybe* coffee afterwards?" His tone lifted at the last, and she nodded, smiling.

"I'll get my coat." She turned around and headed to the small armoire in the corner that housed sweaters and jackets. Inside, everything was neatly folded and color coordinated.

"Wow, I don't think I've ever seen someone so organized outside of the office," he said, looking surprised.

She wondered how many other apartments he saw outside of the office. She wondered what he was thinking now. Maybe he thought she was anal, or she was boring.

"You really have it together, don't you?" He smiled again as she pulled the jacket on over her cute black sundress.

Impressed, he sounded impressed.

"Yeah, I'm a bit of a neat freak." She blushed slightly then turned to grab her purse. "Ready?"

"Yeah, after you." He held out his arm while she switched off the light and locked the door. He pulled the door shut, then reached for her hand.

She felt nervous holding onto his hand and wondered if this was what the *magical sparks* were that she read about in romance novels. She didn't feel electricity, but was sure that's what the authors were always talking about. That kinetic feeling, fireworks…She put her head down, averting her eyes to the elevator buttons. He reached out his left hand and pushed the ground floor.

When they walked out into the street, she couldn't help but notice how beautiful the night sky sparkled. The

42

stars were out heavily tonight as she walked with Kelsey to his car. Although the sky was beautiful, it could never compare to what she was used to at home in Connecticut. She could see more sky there. Here, the beautiful view was blocked. Skyscrapers veiled the picturesque parts of the sunrises and sunsets, and the smog from the larger trucks and constant traffic made it almost impossible to see the beauty of the landscape.

His car was a classic BMW. The exterior was black and the interior was sleek tan leather. It was tidy, complete with a leather bag for trash as well as double "makeup" mirrors. Kelsey checked his twice before they departed.

They arrived at Dominia Paraluccios twenty minutes later. The dress code was upscale. She was glad. He never told her where he was taking her, so she had to guess on the dress code. And luckily, Katherine paid attention to the way he dressed. She had a feeling he would be much the same out of the office as he was in. He would want to impress. So, somewhere fancy.

She was glad that she wore her strappy heels. Kelsey looked great, too. He wore chinos with a black dress shirt and silver tie.

He smiled up at the waitress as she came to the table for their order. He gave her his "signature" look, melting her instantly. She blushed slightly and gave him her full attention. Katherine doubted that any woman who met him could withstand his charm. As the server stood there staring for what seemed like an eternity, she finally looked to Katherine for her order. Kelsey chimed in right away and ordered for them both. She couldn't help but think how presumptuous he was. It was almost something out of that movie, *How to lose a guy in ten days*. He must have thought it was sexy for him to order for the both of them. Strike one. She may not have had a date in a while... too long, but she did know that she knew how to order her own damn meal. She smiled and waited for the linguine with chicken alfredo sauce. The chef's special according to the menu. The problem with being a chef's daughter was the fact that she knew which kind of wine went with which kind of meat. The cabernet was not only the wrong wine to order with the pasta that she was forced to endure, but it was also a very cheap bottle. Everybody knows that a full bodied Chardonnay is the way to go...don't they? So much for Mr. High Fallutin... *Stop finding things wrong with him! He's just being sweet. He's a guy, and he probably doesn't know what wine goes with what....he was just trying to be romantic.* She had to stop thinking altogether and decided that tonight she was going to let loose and have some fun. Besides, she'd been fawning over Kelsey for eight long years.

The server came out shortly and placed their food in the correct places. A complimentary salad sat in front of Kelsey as the server swooned over him. His hand clung to the top of hers as he smiled his thanks. Katherine was aghast; another woman flirting deliberately in front of her; not only did he smile back, but he still held firmly onto her hand.

Katherine cleared her throat. Kelsey's hand snapped back to its previous position as Katherine looked up at the waitress. Her eyebrow arched and a small smirk covered her lips as she walked away and told them to enjoy their meal.

Kelsey turned to the now red-faced Katherine. "I'm sorry if I offended you, Kat. I just wanted to thank the waitress."

"Yes, and did you even order that salad? Is it customary?" she smiled at him from across the table.

"Gees...I thought you were really mad. I'm sorry, Kat. I don't know why she did that." Kelsey laughed as he looked to her. He was sure that the green-eyed monster had captured her and the date would soon be over.

Kat, noticing this, smiled in return and picked up her silverware, twirling the linguine with her fork in her right hand and picked up the glass of cabernet in the other. The pasta wasn't as bad as she thought it would be with the incorrect wine. Growing up with "Chef Gail", she learned the finer things about food and the ways they were prepared. Her mother was a fine cook, attending culinary school in France and doing nothing but waiting on her family hand and foot in the kitchen; it made Katherine appreciate the art of cooking and her mother even more. For this reason, she was particular with what she ordered in restaurants. Cooking at home was always much better, and she picked up on a few things while living on her own. Someday she wanted to cook for her husband and be as good of a wife as her mother.

"You, okay?" Kelsey asked. "You seem a million miles away."

"Oh, no. I'm fine. I was just thinking of my mother." She didn't know why she even told him that. Her nervous energy from the night started to creep up on her.

"Oh, I hope everything is alright... Do you want me to

take you home?" Kelsey looked a little bit concerned.

"Oh, no...nothing like that. I was just tasting the pasta and thinking of my mother. She's a chef."

"Well, I bet you had great meals at home. Is there something wrong with your pasta, then?"

"No, no..." *maybe the wine with the pasta...no, play nice, Kat.*

"Good, I love this place. I come here a lot. I don't think there is anything here that I haven't eaten. I can recommend a few things." He laughed as he caught her eye then started a new topic, "So, How much longer until you leave?

"Ready to get rid of me already?" her tone was light, playful.

Kelsey smiled seductively, "Not quite yet."

What did that mean, not quite yet? She could think of a few things. But the thought sent tendrils of feelings throughout her body, leaving her almost breathless. Kelsey noticed her flush slightly. He smiled at her and turned his gaze downward towards his lasagna. "I'll be leaving Sunday. I've been meaning to thank you for your talk with Janice." She eyed him waiting for his reaction.

"Oh, sorry about that." He put his fork back down, then back to his mouth. "I just thought I would help you out. Sometimes Janice is a little... wiry."

"Well, I appreciate it. At first, I was a little upset with you for saying something. But I really wanted to go out tonight so I didn't think screaming at you would be the right thing to do." She looked at him, smiling again and he returned her gaze. She felt young tonight. First getting jealous of the server, and then mad at him for ordering.

She ruined almost every good thing she had ever been faced with because of her 'standards list'. This was something that her shrink had helped her with. She told her to write down what she wanted in life down to the smallest intricate detail. She did that with everything. That's why she was so neat, so tidy at work, so organized. She used this list with everything from ordering at a restaurant to picking out men and clothing. Everything was perfectly thought out. Eight years she thought about Kelsey, eight years she thought about their first kiss, their first time together. She had a lot vested in him without him even knowing. She wondered if he could feel the same heat across the table that she had been feeling.

They took the last bites of dinner and Kelsey took the bill, leaving the server way over the customary twenty percent. Katherine told herself that he was just a good tipper instead of an insatiable flirt. She stood up with him on her heels helping her with her coat. As they walked out of the restaurant, Kelsey took her hand and led her to his car. The drive was short to the Majestic Movie Theater. It played old black and white movies. She must have had him all wrong. She could never have pictured him taking her to one of these. It was a pleasant surprise when they walked through the door; *Casablanca* was playing. It was one of her favorites. Before the movie even began, however, two young teenagers that sat in front of them were making a movie of their own. Their tongues danced in and out of each other's mouth, obviously not caring who saw them. She and Kelsey were in their seats for less than ten minutes and they were already getting their four dollars' worth.

It had been a long time since she made out with anyone. And never had she made out with anyone in public. It's not that she didn't want to, she did, she just always got the guys who were either too embarrassed or maybe it was the company they were with. She sighed as she watched them continue their public mauling, and took a drink of the coke that Kelsey bought her in the lobby.

"What's wrong?" Kelsey asked amused. Noting the two kids in front of them, she pointed out their position.

"Someday, I want to be like that," she said. Her face turned red as she heard herself say it out loud. "I mean, carefree...Not impersonating a feeding frenzy on animal planet!"

Kelsey laughed then looked at her, "Really?" He leaned in and placed his right hand on her cheek, and pulled her into his mouth for a kiss. His lips were soft. The way his tongue licked her bottom lip made her moan softly, sending a renewed excitement throughout his body. His eyes never left her face, looking into them as he began to touch her.

After an hour long session of serious making out, the movie ended with the two of them giving the teenagers a run for their money. As the credits rolled, catcalls were heard from the back of the movie theatre, and the boy that sat in front of them whose face looked to be sucked off from his girlfriend even commented, "Get a room!" Kelsey smiled and looked at Katherine then grabbed her hand and pulled her out of her seat.

"Well, how was it? Did I live up to your expectations?"

Katherine, red faced, just looked down at the popcorn that lined most of the floor in the theater.

"That good? It was for me as well," he laughed nudging her in the ribs lightly with his elbow. "Coffee?"

Her head finally lifted slightly to a more appealing angle and quickly nodded once. He smiled at her, then took her hand and led her out the double doors of the theater. "I know a place right over here," he said gesturing across the street to a coffee shop with a green and white overhang.

Formosa was a cute little coffee shop on the corner of east and Ninth. The sign was dark red with a coffee cup and a magic wand on the front. The tagline underneath read, 'Our brew is magic'. When they walked in, there were only a few tables left, and luckily for her, they were crammed in a corner. A lone guitarist played some folk music entertaining the young college scene. "Two coffees please, and lots of cream and sugar," Kelsey's voice rang out.

He did it again, he ordered for her. Not only did she like her coffee black with a splash of caramel in it, but she hated when people took the assumption in ordering for her. Strike two. "So, do you bring all of your dates to Formosa?"

"Not all of them, just the beautiful ones."

Forgiven. He knew just what to say and who to say it to. Katherine listened to the guitarist play as he sang his own song entitled, "Forever dazed." She smiled at the lyrics and surprised herself to see that her foot was tapping. Kelsey seemed to enjoying himself, too. After a few minutes in the shop, couples started dancing. Kelsey even stood up and offered his hand to dance. She graciously accepted.

The love song was cute, but not overly cutesy. Kelsey's hand on her waist led her to an appropriate spot on the wooden floor. Surprisingly, Kelsey could not dance whatsoever. His two left feet constantly stepped on hers and he didn't seem to notice that he wasn't at all any good. "I just love to dance," he said excitedly.

"Yeah. Me, too." She smiled in spite of her naked feet to his heel. "Have you ever taken lessons?" she would've snorted if it weren't so unladylike.

"No, I'm just naturally talented."

Yeah, and I'm a football player! "I took a few dance classes when I was younger. My father and I went to a cotillion, and my mother thought it would be beneficial to know how to dance before I embarrassed myself. At the time, I thought it was stupid, but now am grateful for knowing."

The lyrics were being sung out loud by the younger people in the shop.

Living in love, and loving to live
Dying to love a love like this
Wanting to wait, needing this time
Your heart, soul, body and mind
Forever dazed, forever crazed
Your love has left me amazed

So the song wasn't the best, but she was having a good time, bruises and all. After a while of listening to the guitarist, they made their way towards the door, held up by a line of people buying the new artist's CDs. They were stuck behind another couple, who smiled hopelessly at each other.

"Two CD's please," a man said to a woman behind a small folding table. The CDs were sold for five dollars each. He took out a ten-dollar bill and handed it to the woman in charge, then turned around towards the girl who held his attention. "One for you and one for me—our song; I'm having a great time, Lola." The boy smiled sweetly as the girl folded her arms around his neck.

"You're so sweet! Thank you!"

Katherine turned to look at Kelsey. He rolled his eyes and bent towards her ear, "Ten dollars too much."

"I thought it was sweet. Did you see how happy she was?"

"Really? What a waste of money! There's no way that guy back there will ever have a record deal. Come on, let's see if we can get around them before they start making out again," Kelsey said as he grabbed her hand, cramming her through the little walkway out into the night.

***

It didn't take long for her to drift off after she got into her pajamas. The night went as well as to be expected. Other than some of the strikes he received, she did get to kiss him, and it did feel good to be in a man's arms once again. Maybe the next time it would be easier for them. Work would definitely be more interesting.

The next morning when she arrived at work, people seemed a bit cheerier. The hallways were bustling with more people than usual. And everyone was smiling at her as she entered the building. Men were paying attention to her for the first time since she worked here. They must have known that she had a great time last night. They saw her confidence as a woman rise. When she sat down in her cubicle, she received her first phone call within minutes. "Kat, its mom, I had no idea that you were doing a different date column."

"Mom, like I tell you all of the time, it is an advice column, not a date column."

"Well, then, why does it say, 'My date with disaster'?"

If Katherine was surprised by her mom's call, she wasn't surprised after the twenty other calls that were holding on the line for her. Her secretary was bogged down with messages flooding her inbox. "Mom, what are you talking about? I'm not doing a dating column; I just have the same old advice column. Who told you that?"

"Well, Kat, unless you had a date last night and decided to write about it, then you better find out why you are on the *High Fashion* website." Warning lights went off in her head...

"WHAT!" she screamed without even realizing it. She turned on her computer and went straight to *High Fashion* website. She looked at the issue that was to hit this month's newsstands, and there it was. There's no way that this was happening to her. She ruffled through the website when she came to the page, "*My date with Disaster, the Kelsey Martin and Katherine Daniels Love Story.*"

Her face fell in hurt, then twisted in anger. Her skin flushed, "No, no, no!" she repeated. She could hear her mother's voice on the other end of the phone, but couldn't comprehend what to say or do at this moment. The article discussed everything from him ordering for them and her just sitting there like a pathetic person taking it. It also claimed that they were together that night, and "hit a home run," is how he put it. She then read something about how she had hopelessly fallen in love while he did all of the wrong things. He took their date together to sabotage her into a relationship? She then remembered what she thought last night, how the date went just like something out of the movie, *How to lose a guy in 10 days*, and she suddenly felt like a big fool. "Mom, I will call you back. Everything is all right."

"Are you sure, baby? Do you need your father and me to come there?"

"No, mom, everything is fine. I will call you later; right now I have to take care of something."

As soon as she hung up the phone, she started throwing her things in a plastic container that she kept in her work closet.

"Katherine, I am…What are you doing?"

Katherine looked up to see Janice staring at her through her doorway, "I'm packing my things. You obviously have been trying your best to get rid of me. Well, you will have your wish!"

"Katherine, I don't know what to say. I had no idea that was going to be online today. I…"

"Save it, Janice. You're the boss! You're in charge of production! You knew exactly what was going up on the site! If I were you, I would think about getting a good lawyer! When I am done with my lawsuit you may not have a penny in that pretty little account of yours!" Her voice didn't shake as it usually did. She spoke with clear conviction. She felt confident suddenly. Janice's face paled in comparison.

"On what grounds?"

"How does liable sound to you?"

"I don't see how…" Janice's voice faltered.

"I knew something was going on. For weeks, you have been treating me like dirt, then I hear about a pole that you did, saying something like I didn't fit in fashion wise for your stupid ass magazine! You have been jealous since day one. Just because you can't get any other kind of production to see your work, doesn't mean you have to take it out on me. Honestly, Janice, Kelsey? What did you have to give him to write about me?"

Janice's face brightened, "Didn't take much, he wanted to do it, then he started chickening out at the end…I had to assure the idiot to have coffee with you, after your ridiculous make-out session at the movies."

Katherine's face turned red, "How did you know about that? Oh…"

"He called to tell me that he couldn't do this to you anymore, and I assured him that he could keep his job if he could get a good story. He did well, didn't he? I bet the Times won't publish your little articles anymore." She smiled to herself.

"You seem awfully sure of yourself, Janice. Don't you think the higher ups will have a field day with this one?"

"You don't have any proof; besides, a lot of people here know how much you make googly eyes at Kelsey."

"I have all of the proof I need; I can't wait for my lawyer to get a hold of you. Good luck in your writing career. I don't think you will be able to get a job writing jingles when I am through with you." She held up her mini tape recorder and pushed the stop button, then rewound a bit of their conversation for entertainment purposes. When she pushed play and heard the last bit of the conversation, Janice gasped and lunged forward.

"It was all a joke…"

"Save it for someone who cares; now if you please, get the hell out of my cubicle."

CHAPTER THREE

The plane ride to Connecticut from La Guardia wasn't totally unpleasant. Katherine sat in 12b, crammed in the middle of a young couple sandwich, known as Jean and Paul. Jean was a grad student in dance at NYU, and Paul was an architect for Morris Builders in Queens. The two of them met during a small art gallery opening where Paul's sister, Carol, used to work. Their love story was so sweet, and so romantic that Katherine could barely stand to hear it, yet she yearned to be told it repeatedly.

They were perfect for each other, and their attraction was evident from the moment that she sat down between them. They were a beautiful couple. She talked with them about her work with *High Fashion Magazine*. Jean was extremely impressed, as she read *High Fashion* ever since she could remember. She couldn't believe that Kat was the one in the latest article. Paul had offered to beat up Kelsey, and Kat smiled at the thought.

"So, what're you doing going to Connecticut, and why didn't you just drive?" Jean asked curiously.

"Well, I don't have a car, and it's a ways away from my parent's place. And the reason why I am leaving now and not later is because after the article went out, I moped at home. I think Ben and Jerry's had to do a stock inventory." Jean laughed, then smiled reassuringly. "The funny thing is a few days before this whole mess happened, my parents called and asked me to come home to help my father out. It couldn't have happened at a better time really. The thing is, no one knows that I quit *High Fashion*. Well, except for Walter Miller of *Miller, Wade and Thomas*, my lawyer," Katherine put the last part in the familiar hand quotes. "Anyway, so technically, I am jobless, unless The New York Times decides to hire me, which I would take in a heartbeat."

"Damn," Paul said, looking from his girlfriend to Katherine. "Is your father all right?"

"Well, I think so. He has heart problems, but my mom assured me yesterday when I talked to her that the surgery was going to help him, and it was a relatively standard procedure. So, I guess I feel good about that. I suppose I'm insensitive thinking only of myself. It's just been rough. I really liked Kelsey. Eight years of wasting time. You both are so lucky!"

Jean sighed then looked at Paul. It was hard to look at them and hard not to at the same time. Love radiated off the couple, giving her hope for herself.

"I still can't believe what that jerk did that to you," Paul said to Kat. She just shrugged her shoulders and looked towards the back of the seat in front of her. She wished she could change the last week and a half from happening. Date from hell, no job, and now leaving her home for Connecticut. Life sure didn't always turn out rosy. Her father used to say that a lot, and he was right; it sure as hell didn't.

The flight attendant made her speech as the seatbelt light went on. They began their downward descent towards the runway, and soon enough, her family would ridicule her for the article. Her nerves heightened as her two newest friends exchanged phone numbers and emails with her, promising to keep in touch and meet up while she was in Connecticut. It would be a nice diversion during her stay with her folks.

***

Karen Daniels held up a small sign with Katherine's name on it as she descended the walkway from the plane. Kat saw the sign and grinned. "Ha, Ha, very funny, now put that away!"

A nice looking man stood not five feet away as she put her hand on her sister's sign. "Hi," Kat said as she nodded to the man. He smiled back at her and started walking with them. She glanced to the side, and smiled again, then looked at her sister, realizing that this must be the infamous boyfriend.

"Hi, Katherine, I'm Warren." His hand extended and firmly met hers. Her hand was soft, and his was the complete opposite—strong, like surgeons hands. His eyes blazed like fire as he took in her appearance. She blushed slightly. *Get a hold of yourself, Kat; this is your sister's boyfriend, and you know the kind she attracts!*

"It's nice to meet you, Warren. My mother has told me a lot about you and Karen." Warren smiled and Karen laughed. Katherine looked at both of them curiously, "What?"

"You thought *Warren* was my boyfriend? As if!" Karen laughed, and then nudged Warren in the arm. "He's like a brother, that's nastier than incest!" She laughed again as she saw the mortified look on Warren's face. Warren playfully nudged her back.

"Karen, that pretty much is the definition of incest," he joked.

"She never was the brightest bulb in the box." Kat

laughed.

"Nice." Karen smiled.

"Her boyfriend is a lot more *interesting*," Warren said, trying to hold back his laughter. "The last time I saw him, he wore goggles on his forehead while sitting at your mom and dad's dinner table. It was all Bill could do not to laugh!" Karen smacked him once again.

"You both could've been a little less obvious. Besides, they weren't *goggles* they were *Mattoon's,* the newest in fashion. Kat will tell you. It's all over her magazine." As soon as she said it, her sister flinched. "Sorry."

"Hell, I'd apologize, too, Matton's are horrible." Katherine laughed and noticed the eye roll her sister gave her. Her sister and this Warren sure had a good relationship: maybe a gay-best-friend-kind-of-thing going on. She wasn't sure.

"Anyway, Warren's a family friend, actually he's dad's doctor, *and* he reads *High Fashion*." Warren's face reddened. "I'm actually surprised Bill and Gail never mentioned him," Karen droned. She used their first names when she wanted to sound mature.

"I—well, like she said, I read it. I've read your column for a while now. Your father brags about you quite a bit. I thought I'd see what all the hubbub was about." He smiled genuinely.

Hubbub. Yep, definitely dad's doctor. She wondered if he'd read Kelsey's article, too. "Thank you, I'm honored." She smiled as the three of them waited for the luggage return. Warren was a tall man. He looked to be in great shape, he certainly could fill out those khakis and polo shirt. Her body was very aware of how male he was;

practically screaming virile. His scent lingered to her as he helped her with her luggage. Damn she needed to get laid. She laughed to herself.

"I'll help you with those, Katherine," he said as he reached down to pick her luggage up, slightly brushing her shoulder with his left arm. A tingle of electricity made its way up her arm and their eyes met at that moment. He must have felt it, too. The depths of his eyes were like pools of water. The piercing blue she was sure could see right through her. She shivered.

"Here," he said, taking off his coat and placing it around her shoulders. "You must be cold."

She smiled and thanked him. *Cold? Who was he kidding?*

The trio made their way to Warren's car. He had a black *Eddie Bauer* SUV. The inside was tan and had all the bells and whistles that went along with it. He placed her three suitcases in the back along with her overnight bag, then held the door open for her and her sister to get in. Her sister immediately crawled into the back seat and winked at Kat, as she was made to sit in the front passenger seat. Warren's seat was back further than hers was. His legs stretched out in front of him and his right arm lay over the top of her seat as he drove in habit.

"Sorry," he said. His face reddened slightly as they made the left turn into her parent's driveway. She smiled as they pulled up. Her brothers were all there with their families in the driveway, and the front yard was filled with children running amok. A beach ball made its way to the grill of Warrens SUV.

"Oh, God, I'm sorry," Kat winced, then smiled at her nephew that was running toward her vehicle. "He knows better than to—"

Warren's hand covered the top of Katherine's. "It's okay. He's a child. Plus, this wouldn't be the first time that happened, and I'm sure it won't be the last." Warren smiled at her.

That's right, he was a family friend. Funny, she never heard of him. Who knows how many times he had been there before? She felt slightly taken aback. She didn't know that her father's doctor was *that* important in their lives. It wasn't until now that she wondered what was really going on with him. It must've been a lot more serious than she originally thought.

Karen opened her door and got out while Warren and Katherine still sat in the driveway. His hand still covered hers, and she could feel his quickened pulse. She silently wondered if he could feel hers. His touch did something to her. His eyes, still on her, turned downward as he realized he was still touching her. "I…" he seemed to forget what he was going to say.

She would finish it for him. "I need to get out there. I'm sure my parents would like to see me," she said nervously. "Thanks so much for coming to pick me up. I'm sure my sister appreciated your company." *Why would she say that? What would she mention her sister for? She already knew this wasn't goggle man.*

"You're welcome, Kat. I mean, Katherine," he said nervously.

"It's okay. You can call me, Kat. All of my friends call me that," Katherine replied as she opened the door of the truck. "Thanks again."

"I don't want to be just friends," Warren muttered softly when she was out of earshot. It was going to be a long two weeks indeed. With a woman like her around, he would have to keep himself busy. Bill wasn't kidding, she was perfect for him.

***

"Kitty Kat! I'm so glad to see you! Come give your papa a kiss!" Her father had his arms extended as she walked over to him.

"Hi, Daddy," she said happily. "How're you doing?"

"Katie!" William Jr. said. She turned around and her eldest brother ran over to her with something behind his back. Her father gave him a knowing look.

"Billy!" he scolded.

Billy laughed. "Well, Katie, as you know we prepared a hell of a meal for you tonight, a welcome home dinner. Mom made chicken alfredo. I thought this was in order." He handed her the item from behind his back; a bottle of cabernet. *What a jackass.*

"You are such a—"

"Katherine, language!" Gail Daniels interrupted as she slapped her oldest on the side of the head. "Bill, I will deal with you later."

Her other brothers and sister laughed good-naturedly.

"You guy's finished having your fun?" Kat asked heatedly.

"Don't get your panties in an uproar. You know your brothers. If they didn't say something stupid, they wouldn't say anything at all." Her father grinned and continued, "Now, come give me a hug, and tell me where

Kelsey lives. Tommy Jones swears he has a baseball bat with his name on it."

Kat rolled her eyes playfully. "Tommy Jones couldn't hit a t-ball if he wanted to. But, I'll make sure to thank him for the offer." Bill and Gail laughed as a tall, nice looking man came around the corner.

"How exactly are you thanking me, Kitty?"

"Oh, God, you guys really do take in anyone, don't you?" Kat laughed. "How ya doing, Tommy?" Kat asked.

Warren came around the corner now joining in on the fun. He brought a plate of food to the large picnic area in the backyard. From the moment he walked back from his car she caught his eye, he smiled and sat down listening to the banter going on between her and the illustrious Tommy.

"I don't know exactly, maybe I'll think of something." Kat winked and wriggled her eyebrows up and down. The crowd around them oohed and awed. She smiled wider, playing along with the group.

Tommy's face reddened and was smug. "I have an idea, baby...Why don't we go to the movies?" Katherine's face contorted in anger as her fists went to her sides.

"Tommy Jones, I hate you!" she yelled. His smile fell as she lunged herself towards him, wrapping her hands around his neck.

"Whoa, hold on, Kat," Tommy laughed as he tried to catch his breath. "I didn't know you were so wild. I should never have broken up with you, damn!" He chuckled even harder as he fell to the ground with her on top of him. She started to laugh as she loosened her grip.

"Damn it, Tommy," she laughed, "I...I broke up with

you!" She laughed even harder as she sat up clutching her side. Warren and the rest joined in with the laughter. A few minutes later Tommy reached over and planted a big wet kiss on her mouth. Her eyes widened as she realized what was happening. "Oh, God..."

"Tommy," Warren said sternly. Everyone stopped laughing and turned to face Warren. Bill's eyes twinkled as he looked at him. Gail put her hand up to her mouth as to stifle a laugh and Karen and her brothers exchanged glances.

"What?" Tommy said, still laughing. "Oh, gees, Warren. Kat knows I'm just joking. Besides, I'm after the other sister, she's still young." Karen rolled her eyes as everyone laughed.

"Well, that makes sense. I'm not sure if he's a step up or down from the scuba diver," Bill said gleefully. The whole crowd erupted in laughter now as Kat looked at Warren, obviously missing something. She shook it off as she stood up, holding her hand out to Tommy.

"Truce, Loverboy?"

"Why not?" He took her and leaned in to whisper in her ear, "I think Doc's got the hots for ya." Then he walked away, leaving her to turn a bright red, standing by herself.

***

As the day went on, Kat visited with nearly everyone at the family get-together that her parents held for her. The food was great. Her mom prepared all of her favorite dishes as well as some of her famous desserts that she made for the restaurant she worked for. Everyone seemed to be enjoying themselves as they told stories of the past, most of them from Kat's awkward high school dating period, courtesy of the infamous Tommy Jones.

As the night approached, she kissed her nephews goodnight as their families left for home. The only people left were her sister, Karen, Warren and her parents. When the campfire died out, she stood up and began collecting dishes with Warren and Karen as her parents sat at the picnic table chatting. "Damn, Mom is a good cook isn't she, Kat?" Karen said happily as she pat her stomach. Kat looked down at hers, and laughed.

"I'm afraid my buttons will pop! I haven't eaten like that in a long time. Thank God, I'm in New York. I wouldn't be able to resist chez Gail."

Warren smiled as he brought in the last of the dishes and placed them in the sink. "Your mother really outdid herself this time." Karen looked at Kat as Warren picked up a towel to wash the dishes. She motioned with her hands towards his butt, then placed her hands up towards her face and fanned herself theatrically. Kat laughed aloud as Warren turned around. "What? Karen, what are you doing?" Karen's face was red as he looked at her.

"Nothing...I...I'm going to go outside. Kat, won't you dry?" she asked, then winked and threw a towel at her as she walked out the door.

Warren smiled and turned to look at Kat. "You don't have to do any of this, you know? You just got in, and I'm sure you're tired."

"The plane ride was what, an hour?" Kat laughed. "I would feel pretty guilty if I didn't help out. Besides, Karen insisted. I know damn well she won't do it. She never helped out much when we were kids, and if I leave, you will be here all night."

Warren didn't think that was such a bad idea. Sure he had seen pictures of her thousands of times, but in person, she was a knockout. Her personality was great; she was a spitfire with Tommy. He could just about imagine what she would be like in bed. "Well, I appreciate the help then."

The door to the kitchen opened a few minutes later as they were in mid-conversation, about her work with *High Fashion*. Warren quoted a few of her articles and she laughed at some of the advice she gave. Bill Daniels walked in and put his arm around the both of them. "My two favorite people, this is nice," he said, smiling. Kat looked back, the light bulb finally turned on, and she turned around to glare at her father.

"Wait a minute here," she said as she pointed to her father's chest. His face broke into a wide grin with both of his hands coming up in the surrender position.

"What, Kitty? Ah, I missed you so much." He leaned in for a hug, as she awkwardly stood there with her finger still poised.

"Not you, too?" she whispered.

"I don't know what you're talking about, dear. Now, Warren here tells me that he used to take a creative writing course at UCLA, didn't you take something like that?"

Katherine shook her head, not believing the conniving old man. "Yes, of course, but..."

"Katherine, Warren's our guest. You really don't know much about him; besides, I don't know how much longer I can stay up. I'm getting a little tired." He faked a yawn and then turned to look at Warren. "Tell her about the

Creative Writing course, Doc. She can probably help you out." Katherine's father smiled and nudged the young doctor in the shoulder, making a few grunts here and there while he left the kitchen for his bedroom. A few minutes later, she heard the soft sounds of Sinatra coming from the backyard. Her mother walked into the kitchen, smiled, and mouthed "what" when she saw Katherine's face, then walked back toward her bedroom.

"Warren, I'm sorry, I don't know…"

"It's okay, leave it. Besides, I love Sinatra." He smiled, then put his hand on hers as she went to turn towards the backyard. The dishes were almost finished, only a few were left in the sink now. She looked down at their hands and swallowed.

"I'm going to go outside and sit on the dock, I need some air." Warren removed his hand as she walked towards the door.

"I'll come with you." He grabbed a bottle of merlot off the counter with two glasses.

The backyard was lit with little tiki torches that led down to a pond in the very back. Her father and brothers built the dock while she was in high school. They had paddleboats and a canoe tied to the side of it. Warren sat down on one of the Adirondack chairs that sat next to the dock. He placed the bottle of merlot and the glasses on the table that was in-between the two chairs, then looked up to see her hug her arms around her chest.

"This place is great, isn't it?" Warren picked up the wine and poured them each a glass.

"Yes, it's nice. I had a great childhood. Do you live

around here?" she asked, now turning towards her chair to sit down. Warren handed her a glass of the merlot, and then took a seat beside her. "Thanks."

Warren nodded. "Yes, actually I live within walking distance. I have a house about a mile away from here, but I love the pond. Your dad and I sit out here for hours sometimes just talking."

"Really? I didn't know dad was doing so badly; I had no idea that you saw him so much."

"Oh, not professionally, although your dad should be more careful with his health, he'll be just fine. I, on the other hand, think I need him more than he needs me. I was never able to talk to my parents the way I can talk with him and Gail. He seems to know me better than I do... at least knows what's good for me." He smiled, then looked up to find her staring at him; he glanced back down immediately.

"Wow, I don't think I've ever had that kind of relationship with my dad. I can talk with him, but I guess I close myself off. Now my mom, on the other hand, we have shared some secrets." She chuckled, thinking of all of the times she and her mom laughed about men.

"Yeah, Gail's great. I had a few bad days in the past month and your dad brought me out here on the water to clear my head." Why was he telling her this? He hadn't so much confided in his own mother. He seemed like a faucet around her, pouring out his thoughts.

"Oh, I'm sorry to hear that. My dad used to bring me out here to fish when I was younger. It's peaceful, helps with the thinking. I hope you're doing well now?"

"Yes, much better, thanks. Hey, would you be

interested in going out there for a little while?" He gestured to the lake.

"Well, I…"

"You know, it's okay if you don't want to. I just thought all this talk about the water, you know… forget it."

"I think it would do me a little good. I'm coming off a bad week myself. Wanna go get some poles? I'll untie the boat." She smiled as she stood up, stretching and taking in the cool night's breeze.

"Sure." Warren stood up and went up to the house to collect the poles and tackle box.

As he made his way down from the house, she noticed his hands shaking slightly. He seemed nervous. "I brought some mosquito repellent, too…" He sounded like such a dork.

"Thanks, I was hoping you would bring that. I used to get bitten to death out here." He dropped the stuff down into the canoe and reached up for her hand as she shakily stepped in. The boat rocked slightly, and then she fell into his arms.

Arms that felt so good to fall into.

The heat inside her started to well up as she steadied herself for more deadly waters. She looked up and saw him staring back down at her lips. It was then that she knew he was going to kiss her. He tilted his head lower and brought his hands up to her jaw, bringing her lips to his. His tongue outlined her mouth, then he took her bottom lip in his and kissed her.

Her lips were soft, inviting, as he took in the sweet taste of her.

She didn't want to pull back, but something made her.

She looked up, wondering if it felt just as good for him as it did for her, and then she saw him smile.

He could still feel the way her lips felt against his, the way she felt when they touched. He was still touching her, holding on to her tightly. Then a light shone in the distance, breaking the hold that he had on her and he realized it was a porch light.

Her heart beat quickly as she stood there, thinking about what just happened. Warren put his hands to his side as she slowly backed away. "Maybe this was a bad idea." Her face turned pink as she climbed out of the boat. "Thank you for the kiss... I mean the boat, the... thank you."

Warren smiled. She was flustered, and he got her that way. He felt it, too. He bent down to sit in the boat, feeling the back of his neck with his hand. He shook his head. He knew from the months that he had known her father that she was a special lady. Her father talked about her likes, dislikes, her schooling, then recently he told him that he was worried for her in the big city. And, somehow, so was he. New York certainly had its ups, but had a lot of downs, too. As far as crime went, it was everywhere. But now that he had met Katherine, he could tell why Bill had been so worried. She was nothing like he had ever known. She was something else.

He decided that he now needed that boat ride more than ever. From the moment she got off of the plane and walked with him and her sister, he felt like he'd been hit by a Mack truck. The woman that he'd dreamed about for months was finally there, and she was everything that Bill said she was and more. After kissing her, he knew that he had to do it again. He sat on the boat for a few hours, thinking of his strategy for just that. Once he felt confident that a good plan was made, he stepped out of the boat and drove home.

Bill Daniels watched the doctor from his bedroom window. He saw him in the boat, he saw the kiss, and smiled. It wouldn't take much to get those two together, he thought. All it needed was a little push. Katherine was a tough egg to crack; they butted heads a lot when she lived at home, but God how he loved her. She was the only one of his kids that he felt confident would survive outside of the home. Bill shook his head and laughed as Gail turned her head from her pillow. "What are you doing up this hour, Bill?"

"Oh, the boy just kissed her. I didn't think he would ever make his move; thank God I didn't tie that boat securely to the dock the last time I went out. You should have seen it. She practically… well, she did. She fell into his arms, and what did I tell you… fate. Those two are meant to be together. A doctor, Gail!" He wiggled his eyebrows like his daughter, and happily cried, "Free health care!"

"Oh, God, Bill. You're as bad as Aunt Tilly. Let the girl fall in love with who she wants to." Gail smiled then made her way to the window. "Where is she now?"

"Ah, she went to bed. She came in after the porch light went on." Gail turned her head now to look at her husband.

"Porch light? The *motion* detector?"

"I'll be dammed if I wanted to get a closer look, and I forgot about the damn sensor… rookie mistake."

"Aunt Tilly would be embarrassed." Gail shook with

laughter.

"Come here, Gail," Bill growled. "I'll show you..."

Gail laughed as Bill brought her to the bed.

CHAPTER FOUR

Warren was up for what seemed like hours when his bedside alarm went off. He pushed the button and stood up just as the phone on the stand rang. "Hello, this is Warren."

"Warren, my boy," a man's voice sounded on the other end. Warren smiled and inhaled.

"Bill."

"Any plans for today, son?" Bill Daniels' voice rang out.

"Uh, actually, I have a few things that I wanted to get done today, other than that, nothing. You know I'm on vacation this week. Whatcha need?"

"Oh, nothing... Well, I just thought I would call to see if you would help Katherine out. She was talking about you all last night, you know?"

Somehow, Warren knew Bill was exaggerating as usual. After seeing Katherine's face turn that shade of pink, he figured she went straight to bed. "Really?" he said sarcastically.

"Yeah, you must have impressed her with that creative writing class. She chatted until the cows came home," Bill said loudly, playing it up as he playfully nudged Gail with his elbow. She rolled her eyes at his excited grin.

"She did, huh? I didn't... we didn't... well she," he stammered. When he got around this family, his mind seemed to get the case of the nerves. Mr. Daniels chuckled then started in again.

"Don't worry, Doc. It was all good. She's in the living room right now with her sister. Why don't you come on over. You know you want to."

Warren's face tinged with red. Bill Daniels knew exactly how to get him.

The fact that Bill was playing matchmaker with his own daughter made Warren feel special for some reason. He'd been through a lot lately and Bill knew that.

"I'll be over in a few minutes."

"I knew you would come to your senses. Now, the story is, she needs a ride to the post office."

"The post office? Really, Bill? Come on, it's only a block from the house." Warren chuckled as he moved around his bedroom getting dressed.

"Hey, you know the solution, don't you? Think of a better lie. Now, don't let her know I called you, okay?"

"Alright, Bill. I'm hanging up now." Warren hung up the phone and shook his head, that sly old man was something else.

A few minutes after he hung up, Warren was driving down to Katherine's. This wasn't exactly what he came up with last night, but hey, it did get him here. He was sure he could come up with something better than the post office. He tapped lightly on the door as he saw her walk past the refrigerator through the side window.

She peeked through, feeling slightly nervous; she quickly turned around, brushed her hair back behind her ears with her fingers and pushed down the front of her blouse, making sure all the buttons were intact. "Coming," she said, and opened up the door.

"Good morning, Katherine."

"Good morning, Warren. My dad isn't here; he just left, but if you want you can come in." She smiled as she stepped to the side and let him through. Great, now what? He was definitely going to have to use the stupid post office excuse.

"Your father called, he asked if I could drop you off at the post office. He said you also needed a few things in town as well." Bill wouldn't be pleased about this. Hey, if he was going down, he was sure as hell going to drag him down with him.

He did, did he? Sly old man, "I don't want to put you out, Warren. My father can sometimes be a bit pushy when it comes to his daughters." She smiled at the last of her words, "I am sure that you have to be at work, you know, saving lives and all."

"Actually, as luck would have it, I'm on vacation now. I was supposed to go fishing with your dad this week. Today, actually, I'm surprised he isn't here." He hated to lie, but didn't have much of a choice. He wanted to be there.

"Really? Aren't you his heart doctor? He told me he was having heart problems...What's going on here?

Uh, oh. "Hey, I can't say anything to you about your dad's health...privacy laws..."

"You can't tell me anything?" Warren shook his head no. "Okay, well, I guess I will take you up on the post office." Figuring there was no need to argue, she asked, "Would you like something to drink?"

"Yes, that would be nice." He followed Katherine into the kitchen. He wondered if he should mention anything about the night before, but decided against it.

"So, about last night," Katherine said quickly, "I'm not sure we should have..."

"You regret it?" Warren said quietly.

"No," she said softly, Warren exhaled. She looked at him. "It's just that... I don't think it should happen again. I mean, I'm going back to my life in New York; you live here, and besides, you're a family friend. It might not work out, and then you will have lost your friendship with my father. I wouldn't want that to happen." She said the last bit quite fast, and Warren was still processing what she was saying.

"Oh, well...I guess there's not much to say to that." He scoffed. "I'm not sorry it happened."

"You're not?" she asked, surprised.

Warren looked at her as if she was crazy, "Hell no. I was up all night thinking of a way to ask you out, but I can see that that was pretty much for nothing." She smiled, and her eyes sparkled. Damn they were beautiful. "What?" he asked, noting the humor in her eyes.

"Nothing, I... I needed that." She smiled. "Thank you."

"You're welcome," he hesitated. He didn't know if she wanted him to ask her out or to kiss her again, or what. So, he led the way into the living room and sat down with his glass of water. "Thanks for the drink. I didn't know where you wanted to go for shopping, but I thought maybe the ..." At that moment, two things happened. Kat walked around the couch to sit down, tripped over Warren's legs, and fell right into his lap. Her water went everywhere; she flinched and looked up with horror on her face. "Hey, you," Warren whispered.

"I... I'm sorry."

"Don't be," he said softly, looking down at her lips. He watched them part slightly then he tipped her chin up and met her for a kiss. Her eyes closed as he kissed her. Her body felt like it would give out; his hands now went to her waist as he brought her into him. Her arms moved up and her hands twined around his neck. He brought his lips to her neck, sending little nibbles down her flesh. She moaned softly, the sound of it sent trembles down his body.

She slowly moved her hands down his chest and pushed him down on the sofa. He was on his back when the doorbell rang. They both quickly sat up, knocking them out of the trance.

"Oh, my God," Katherine said.

"Wow," Warren exhaled.

"Door," she said.

"Right."

"Can you get it?" she asked, flushed.

"Not, exactly," he replied; his face was flush, and she noticed him place one of the throw pillows on his lap.

"Oh." She giggled. "Right, I'll get it." Warren nodded. Kat took a deep breath, straightened her clothes, and then braced herself for the door.

"Oh, God," she muttered. "Tommy, hi, how are you doing? Elliot isn't here," she quickly ventured. Tommy's eyes found hers, and then looked down once for good measure and back up again. A wide grin formed on his face, then he glanced over to the living room where he saw Warren on the couch.

Warren saw the exchange and vowed silently to himself to get him back one way or the other. Tommy laughed.

"Warren, hi, how ya doing?" Tommy joked.

Warren glared up at him, "Doing well, Tommy, you?"

He wondered if Tommy ever got rid of that mysterious rash. Now would be a perfect time to bring it up, but deciding it was unethical to mention, he kept it to himself.

"Just fine, just fine," he muttered. "Katherine, I wasn't looking for Elliot, I thought you might need a ride around town."

Kat laughed. "Well, I know my dad didn't call you." Warren laughed aloud.

Tommy looked confused. "What are you talking about?" He noticed her red face and swollen lips, and a sly smile spread across his face. He looked back at Warren, who was still on the couch. The TV was off, and he saw the strategic placement of the blue, turquoise throw pillow. He laughed.

"Katherine Elizabeth Daniels, am I interrupting something?" Tommy asked in his best Gail-voice.

Katherine noticed how bad the situation might look, then went over to the couch and grabbed the pillow off Warren's lap and tossed it at Tommy's head. "Get out of here, Tommy. I didn't want it back then, and I still don't want it now!"

He infuriated her. He got under her skin like a tick. Tommy laughed the entire way out the door. Katherine turned and walked towards Warren.

"Warren, I'm sorry, I didn't mean to jump you back there, and it's not like me to be…"

He smiled then motioned her towards the couch. "You keep apologizing."

"I know," she whispered.

"Don't."

She smiled as he reached out and grabbed her hand. "I

78

feel like a kid making out on my parent's sofa. Not that it wasn't great, it's just… We're adults for God sake." She started to laugh, thinking of her brothers and how they always made sure they bought their dates dinner first—an incentive for making out, made sense.

"What's so funny?" he asked curiously.

"Oh, uh nothing, I was just thinking to myself."

"Oh? What were you thinking?"

"Well, I don't know what's gotten into me. First last night, then the couch, and oh, my God, Tommy is going to tell everyone. Listen to me, like I'm worried what that idiot's going to say. I just know I can't do this at my parent's house."

"Wanna go to my house?"

Kat looked at his face. He was teasing her…*what the hell*? "Yes."

He looked taken aback. "Well, then…my kind of girl." He laughed as he pulled them both to their feet and dragged her through the doorway out to his car.

CHAPTER FIVE

Minutes later, they arrived at a large home on the corner of Fifth and Rosedale. She loved the area. It wasn't quite in the city, but not in the Boondocks either. The street was familiar. She remembered it from when she lived back home. Her friend Keri Smith lived at the house across the street from Warren's. She wondered if Keri's parents still lived there.

His house was a Tudor style home, with a beautifully landscaped lawn and a cute lamppost at the end of the drive that welcomed people as they pulled in. She couldn't believe only one person lived there.

"I used to ride my bike here all the time. Well, to the house across the street."

"Really? When you were a kid?"

"No, last week..." Kat laughed and elbowed him. "Of course when I was a kid."

"I see how you are. You say you aren't like Bill, huh? Well, I got news for you," he joked back as he opened the door to his house.

It was nice. It looked lived in, not scary like her New York apartment. You could most certainly tell he had a good job. Artwork lined the walls in the kitchen, and he had a beautiful pot and pan rack hanging over the large island in the middle. The same Van Gogh print that she had in her apartment hung in the dining room above a nice cherry buffet.

He placed his house keys on a hook beside the refrigerator, then looked up at her. "Would you like something to drink?"

"No thank you. I'm... I don't know... I don't know what I'm doing here! I just met you yesterday. I usually don't do things like this," she said nervously, pacing the kitchen.

"It's fine. You don't have to be nervous about anything, Katherine," Warren said, walking over to her, touching her shoulders.

She could feel his warm hands brand her skin; she glanced up to his face, and she knew he meant it.

"Now, let's get to know one another," he said smiling. He grabbed her hand and led her to the living room. "What would you like to know? That seems like a bit too much for now; how about four questions?" He smiled as she scrunched up her nose in thought. Everything about her was so damn cute.

"Four questions, huh?" She smiled jokingly. "Okay, question number one. Are you operating on my father this week? This all seems like a setup to me, an ambush. I came here because my mother couldn't get off at the restaurant for it."

Warren narrowed his eyebrows in thought, *Surgery? Bill has been a little run down lately, but nothing serious like she was letting on.* He wondered if there was something Bill wasn't telling him. He wondered if there was something else wrong medically that didn't have to do with his heart. When he didn't speak quickly, Kat rolled her eyes.

"Ah ha, I knew it! You're in on this, too, aren't you? He isn't even sick! What kind of scheme are you both trying to pull?" Her hands were on her waist, much like a mother would do before she scolded a child. She was furious.

"Whoa, wait a minute. I'm not in on any kind of

scheme, or games. I'm not into games. Whatever Bill told you is his business, and like I said before, I can't divulge any health information; I could lose my license. I can tell you that your father's health would be a hell of a lot better if he would start following his diet a lot more. You know how your father is—stubborn."

Well, that much was true. Bill Daniels never liked to be told what to eat and what not to. "You're sure about this?" she asked, being skeptical.

"Positively."

"Ok, sorry. I guess I'm just overly paranoid right now." She shook her head and faced him again, getting ready for question number two.

"So, does any of this paranoia stem from the Kelsey incident?" He hated to even mention that creep, but he didn't want to be compared to scum.

She took a deep breath then shrugged her shoulders. "I suppose so. You have no idea what I've been through. I had a thing for him for eight years. I'm... I'll be honest, embarrassed. And, I'm not looking for a relationship, that's for sure." After she said it aloud, she realized that she didn't really mean it. Warren winced.

"You know, not all men are like him." His temper rose as he spoke to her. His eyes darkened to a darker blue as he spoke. "I don't like him one bit."

"Well, as it happens, you're not alone in that department. I—" She almost let the cat out of the bag. She quit. She definitely wasn't ready for her parent's to find out about that yet. "I don't like him much either."

"Well, you know your parents are glad to have you here. They talk about you all the time."

"Yeah, I suppose so. I miss them, too." *Not enough to move home though.* That's all she needed, everyone to find out what kind of failure she was with no job and all.

"You could make more time for them. Give them some credit, Katherine. You haven't been here since last Christmas." Even as he was saying it, he knew he didn't have a right.

"What? Are you kidding me? I talk to them all the time on the phone. I live in New York; you know, the roads run both ways, and furthermore, how is that any of your business?" she said heatedly then got up and walked toward the kitchen.

"Katherine, wait. I'm sorry. I don't know what's gotten into me." He lowered his gaze then reached out for her arm.

"Let go of me. I don't need someone telling me that I haven't spent enough time here. I lived here almost my whole life. I needed air, and I needed space. I never got that when I lived here. As much as I love my parents, I... You know what? Forget it."

"Katherine, please don't go. Katherine," Warren pleaded as she walked out the door. Ran was more like it. He went to follow her, but figured it was best that he just stay away for now. After all, her parents' home was only a mile away, not very long for a woman who was used to walking everywhere. What the hell was he thinking yelling at her? She didn't even... he couldn't even finish the thought.

He'd been thinking of Katherine Daniels for some time now. Her father brought in pictures to the office, talked about her as if Warren had known her for years. He felt like they were dating, for Christ sake. He knew practically everything there was to know about her; her favorite color, flower, and perfume. Just the smell of her was toxic to his already tightened nerves. He couldn't stand in the same room with her without thinking of touching her.

When he finally saw her at the airport his whole world seemed complete. *But she still didn't know him.* He wanted to tell her tonight. The perfect moment would have happened tonight—he hoped while she asked about him, that he would find the courage to tell her. She didn't even know about his wife. How in the hell was he going to explain that one? "By the way, Katherine, I have a wife, her name's Sarah," he scoffed. How in the hell do you tell someone that you think you're falling in love with them, then tell her you have a wife at the same time? Life is a son of a bitch. He didn't know who ever said that, but they were right. He'd been too chicken to tell her the details on that relationship, and now he lectured her on that stupid ass that wrote an article on her, not to mention the fact that she was a lousy daughter? He knew that she was far from that. He knew she talked to Bill and Gail every day; Bill constantly bragged about it. He knew about the letters she sent to them, or the plane tickets she sent a few different times, even though the drive to New York was shorter than the plane ride and the hassle at the airport.

Irritated with himself, he shook his head and grabbed his coat; he had to apologize to her, and calling her wouldn't do much. She probably wouldn't pick up the phone.

Then the phone rang.

"Hello."

"Warren, my man, this is Bill. Kat just walked into the house all up in arms. What happened?"

Bill was his joking self, but something in his tone sounded fatherly, like he was about to get his butt kicked.

"I'm sorry, Bill. I don't know what came over me. I mentioned that idiot, Kelsey, and then I started in on her for not visiting you and Gail."

"What the hell would you do that for? That's not even romantic. You need to watch one of those chick flicks with her; that'll soften her up. Do you want me to ask Gail which one to get?"

The man gave awful advice on women, that much he knew for sure. "No, Bill. I don't think this is as simple as a chick flick fix. I was just on my way over to apologize."

"Well, if you're sure. Now, don't you go feeling bad. You're perfect for my Kat, she just doesn't know it yet. That idiot Kelsey had to screw things up. Now, just remember what I told you about mentioning things like that. Don't be a pinhead."

"Now we're resorting to name calling?" Warren laughed.

"Don't you worry about it." Bill chuckled. "Now we need to think of plan b."

"Plan b? You're ridiculous; did I ever tell you that?" his smile grew as he listened to Bill.

"Someone has to be the brains of this operation, and for being a doctor you would think it would be you, but I digress... Flowers. Kat loves 'em. Her favorites were always Irises. I'm taking her mother out this evening. She should be here by..."

"*Dad?* Are you on the phone? I thought we were going

fishing? Come on," Kat called from the other room. She sounded better. She probably already forgot about him.

"I'll be there in a minute, sweetheart. I'm just talking to Aunt Tilly. Yes, yes Tilly, I'll take her out tonight at eight. Dinner, yes… Love you, too. Don't forget what we talked about."

Clever old man. Warren had two hours to get ready for the big apology. Shower, dress, and flowers. He'd better hurry.

"Uh, ok… Bill, wait. What's this about you needing a surgery, did you get another doctor?"

Click.

The receiver went dead, and Warren wondered what Bill was up to.

Eight o'clock came, and Warren stood before the door to Kat's parents' house feeling foolish. He hoped her father was right about what to do; the flowers, stopping by like this. He reached out to knock on the door when the door opened, and she walked out, almost running into him. She looked beautiful, angelic. The white sundress blew in the cool air. Her long brown hair cascaded in curls that flowed down her back.

"Oh!" Her hand went to her heart. "You startled me. What are you doing here?"

He held out the flowers and spoke softly, "I'm sorry about earlier."

Her face was cold as stone. "Accepted. Now, I have to get going. Mom and Dad aren't here right now. They should be back later this evening. You better try them in the morning." She stepped past him down the stairs and walked towards the lake.

"Katherine, please. I'm sorry. I don't know what I was saying. I know you love your parents. I just—"

"You don't know anything," Katherine interrupted. "You don't know me, Warren, so don't pretend to. As much as I like you, you can't just come into my life the way you think you can! You can't tell me what to do, tell me how to act, or make me feel the way you do. It's..."

"You like me?" He desperately clung to the hope that she may have had a feeling... something.

"You misunderstood." Somehow when she said that she knew that it was a lie, but she didn't care. She wanted to hurt him like he hurt her.

"Well, I *am* sorry." He shook his head then said, "I'd better leave you to your evening." He turned away and walked towards his car. He was madder than anything right now; mad at himself for liking her so much, mad because he made a fool out of himself.

She held onto the irises that he gave to her, then looked over to the driveway where he stood. He came to apologize. It must have taken a lot to come over. She felt awful. How could a man that she just met know her like he did? "Warren, stop!"

He ran his hand down his face and turned to face her. She walked over to him and placed her hand on his shoulder. The same feeling, the spark, came over her. "Warren, I..." She brought her hand up to his face, dropping the flowers to the ground. Her lips found his in an instant. He sighed as she took his bottom lip in her mouth, crushing herself up against him. It felt natural to kiss him, almost as if they were made for each other. "I'm sorry."

He smiled at her and pulled his arms around her tight, "I'm sorry, too."

***

The woman was smiling in her sleep, only she didn't show the emotion. She could see places and time, she could hear things that went on around her, she could feel when someone touched her, but she couldn't say anything, and she couldn't let people know that she knew, heard, smelled, or thought.

It was as if she was floating on the outside of her body, somewhere between heaven and earth. She was neither alive nor dead, but she supposed more of a spirit floating around and waiting for her time to bide before taking her final step towards heaven.

She smiled down at the woman and man, noticing that he was taken with her. She was glad that she found her for him. She set their paths in motion. She wanted him to be happy. She would have leapt for joy if she could have. Now, it was her time; she could feel it. She knew they would be okay together, so she let her body relax and her breath float to the space between both worlds.

"I'm ready," she said with clear conviction. The light shown in through the window of the quaint room, and her soul soared up through it. She felt the way she did when she got married, when she made love with her husband; she basked in the light, and in her love for him, then the monitor flat lined, and she passed.

***

Warren and Katherine stood, embracing. He felt for one moment, that his life might actually be moving on inally. After five years of heartache, he finally felt able to breathe. The buzzing from his cell phone in his pocket brought him back. He tore away from their embrace, "Katherine, hold on, I have to take this."

Kat smiled up at him, and pulled her hair away from her face. He stood there by his car, looking so amazing. His kiss was still sending sparks of life down her body. She liked the way he held her. She felt calm, wanted. Then she noticed his body tense. He started pacing back and forth by his car. His arms went up above his head, not in anger, but he looked pained. Tears started exploding from his eyes. She didn't know what to do. Should she comfort him? She wasn't good with men crying. It tore at her heart. "Warren, are you okay?" she asked softly.

"I...I—." he felt his knees give out as he slumped down to the ground. The cell phone that he held seconds before lay on the ground now by his feet.

Katherine went to him. "Warren? Are you okay? Warren, Warren," she said while she nudged him. He didn't move. His face went blank. She picked up the phone and looked at it. Maybe she could call the number back.

Nothing.

The phone was dead.

She pulled own her own phone and dialed 911.

***

The emergency room was filled with the usual sights and sounds: people running amok, ambulance sirens cut through the air, doctors running down the halls with clipboards. Kat sat at Warren's side in room 203, waiting for the doctor to come in. His eyes seemed unable to focus on anything.

The doctor came in. "Warren, are you okay? What happened?" He snapped his fingers a couple of times in front of Warren's face. Warren blinked, but didn't feel like answering. "Miss, could you tell me what happened to him?"

"No, I don't know. He was talking on the phone. He got a phone call, I don't know—"She was hysterical; her words all ran together. The doctor's hand went to hers.

"Ma'am, it's okay. I need you to take a deep breath and think about what happened. Are you okay?"

"Yes, sorry, I just...phew! He got a phone call, I don't know who from. I went to check on his phone, but nothing came up. Then he just fell down. I tried talking to him, but nothing. I'm sorry; I really don't know what happened."

The doctor looked at her and then shook his head. It seemed like he figured out something, then he walked out to the nurses' station. She could hear him ask the nurse something about a woman named Sarah. All she heard was the word "wife" and "hospital". He couldn't have been married. Her father would never have pushed her towards a married man. She didn't know Warren that well, but surely she knew him well enough that he wouldn't cheat on a wife? She turned and looked at Warren, then the Doctor came back in.

"Excuse me, did you say *wife*?" She looked up at the two conversing in the doorway. The doctor's voice seemed paler.

"Ma'am, I can't discuss that with you, if he hasn't. You're obviously not family." He said more as a statement than a question. *And there it was.* He must've been married. It all made sense now. The house was excessively big for one person, but why would he bring her to his home? This was some kind of a sick joke.

"If you know his family, you should give them a call. He's going to need them now. He'll be fine physically. But, I'll be back in a few minutes to check on him." The doctor nodded then left the room. She turned to look at Warren.

"Warren, it's me... Katherine." She nudged him lightly. "I'm going to get your wallet, okay? I need to find some phone numbers. Do you have any?" she asked.

He nodded his head in agreement, as he handed her his wallet. She opened it, noticed his insurance card, and then found a small list of phone numbers. "Is this your family?" she asked, noting a few Connecticut area codes.

"Yes."

Then she found his pictures. He had one picture of a woman in his wallet; it must have been his wife. "Warren, should I call..."

"Sarah, her name is Sarah," he said between sobs.

She didn't know whether to be mad or how to feel. She looked at him to continue, but he didn't say anything.

"Should I call her? Does she have a cell?" she asked, trembling. She had messed around with a married man, and now she was sitting in here. She was going to have to call his wife.

"She's already here. She's upstairs. She..." He stammered through his words, his thoughts, his hands went to his head and pulled his hair; tears flowed as she looked at him. "I'm sorry, Katherine."

"You should be. You had a wife and you were kissing me! That's not really important now. Just tell me where she is, and I will go get her. She should be here for you, not me," she said, frustrated.

Then her phone rang.

"Dad. Yes, I'm okay. Yes, Warren is with me. No, we're at the hospital. I think you better get here right away."

The receiver went dead and she flipped her phone closed. Her attention went back to Warren. "Tell me where she is, Warren, and I will go up and get her."

"She's dead."

Surely she didn't hear him right. "Dead? Warren, how do you?" She thought about the phone call, the devastation in his eyes, and she didn't know what to do. "Warren, were you still married? This wasn't an *ex*-wife?"

"Yes, I was still married," is all he could muster.

She now could feel her eyes burning beneath the lights. *He had been kissing her while his wife was dying.* She didn't know what to do. She felt angry, but she felt awful like she should be comforting him. She didn't know what to say, what to do. She was going to wait until her parents got there. Surely they didn't know he was married?

"I'm sorry, Warren. I'm so sorry." She put her hand over his and he held onto it tightly; he squeezed once then took a deep breath. Her father walked in minutes later. Warren stood up from the bed as Bill came around the bed and brought him into his embrace.

"I'm so sorry, Warren. I know how difficult this must be for you. I'm so, so, sorry. How are you holding up?" Warren still clung onto him tightly. Katherine's mother was brushing tears from her face as she looked at the two men. She went over to Warren, too, and gathered him into a hug, kissing his forehead.

"Are your parent's on the way?" Bill asked.

"I haven't called them yet," Warren choked. "I need to call Grace and Evan; they will be devastated."

Bill nodded, "We will give you some privacy."

Katherine just shook her head; she was shocked to say the least. Her parents knew he was married? They'd been pushing her towards him since her arrival yesterday afternoon. She thought they were. *Oh, God. Maybe they weren't!* What kind of person was she?

"Katherine, I," Warren managed to mutter a few words to her as he saw her start for the door. He couldn't seem to concentrate.

"It's okay, Warren. I'm okay. I will pray for Sarah," she said, holding back the tears then opened the door and walked towards the waiting room. Katherine's mother, Gail, looked at Warren and realized what was going on.

"Warren, I better go check on her, are you going to be okay?"

"Yes, please, go after her." He worried for Katherine. He never meant to hurt her. He felt just like that asshole, Kelsey. She would never forgive him for not telling her the whole truth; she would probably be on the first plane back to New York.

"Katherine, are you okay?" Gail asked her daughter when she caught up to her.

"I...What the hell were you all thinking? You were pushing me towards a married man!" She yelled in the emergency room waiting area. People walking in and out stopped to watch the show as they came into the room.

"Katherine, I'm sorry. It's really a sensitive situation. You see...Warren has been married for eighteen years..."

"Eighteen years? Oh, that's just perfect. I'm glad he's a real stickler for vows!" she shouted.

"Sarah, has been in a coma for the last five," her mom said slowly.

Katherine stopped; she closed her eyes and turned towards her mother.

"In a coma?"

"Yes. He's been alone this whole time. He's been very attentive to her. He still visits her every day, but nothing, and I mean nothing could bring her out of it. The doctors all have told him that. He just couldn't do it. He couldn't pull the plug. Five years ago, she overdosed on some medication. She'd just found out that she couldn't have children, and decided to take her own life. Warren walked in after work and discovered her on the floor. He called the hospital, and they pumped her stomach, but could do nothing else. She was alive, but in a vegetative state. He couldn't bear to take her off life support. Up until last year, he didn't see anyone. He just started working again, talking again. Your father has taken to him a bit. Warren comes over often, fishing with your father. They talk, Katherine."

Katherine's tears flowed freely down her face; she bit back the tears enough to speak, "My God, Mom, that..."

"I know. He wanted to tell you; I could tell by the way he looked at you. He wanted me to come out here to get you. He's a good man, Katherine. We wouldn't have done any of this if we didn't think so. We should have told you about her, but we didn't think that was our place."

"I can't deal with anything like this, Mom. I... this is just way too heavy for me right now. He seems wonderful, but... Why would she try to kill herself? Why the hell would somebody do that?" As she said that, she felt odd. She felt awful, ashamed.

"I don't know. As you can imagine, he's been through hell. Please go easy on him." Her mother looked concerned.

"I..." She shrugged. "Of course I will. What kind of woman do I look like? Jesus, Mother."

Gail winced at her language, then turned back towards Warren's room, watching as Katherine walked out the door.

CHAPTER SIX

Three days later, Katherine lounged in the Adirondack chair on the boat dock, reading her mail. She got a few letters from Janice, apologizing for the whole "incident" as she liked to call it. Yeah, right. Like she would believe anything that bitch said. She read another letter from her lawyer, stating that she had a good case against *High Fashion* with a possible settlement deal, and he would keep in touch. It looked promising. And, since she didn't have a job anymore she would most likely take them up on her offer. Another letter was from Kelsey, asking when and if she was coming back. *Loser*, she thought. Then she saw it: a pay stub. Her article was going to be in the Times any day now. She smiled, hoping her advice would help the troubled man.

Suddenly, shivers crawled up her neck.

She bolted straight up with a gasp. She had known Warren longer than she had thought. She had known him for months now; he was *Confused in Connecticut!*

Oh, no! She ran up to the house and ran right into her father. "Katherine, wow! It's great! Probably your best yet, and in the *Times*! I'm impressed," her father said with his newspaper unfolded before him.

"It's in today's paper?" Her face looked pained. "Oh, no, Warren! Give me that!" She grabbed it. Bill gave her a scolding look.

"I wasn't done with that!"

"You are now! Oh, God!" There it was "Advice for the lost," by Katherine E. Daniels, with her picture sitting proudly beside the title. She brought her hand up to her

96

hair and shook her head.

She read.

Dear Katherine,

I am sick of the pity, the looks that I get from people who find out. The way I feel when I go out in public, like people are staring, judging me, wondering what I did to make her do what she did. My wife committed suicide. Only worse, she didn't die. She sits in the hospital hooked up to machines.

On the outside she was the happiest woman in the world, she was my rock. She was the love of my life. We were married for thirteen years when she did it. She took pills, and lots of them. She'd just found out that she was unable to have my children, our children, and she apparently couldn't think of any other way to go on. She never thought about what I felt on the subject. She didn't think about adoption, foster care, surrogacy, she didn't think of anything! She was selfish, something that I never would have thought of my Sarah, the love of my life.

What she did that day ruined my life, and took out all hope for a future for myself, until I found a voice, an angel to help me through all of the pain. It has been five years since she decided to do this. She still sits in the hospital, catatonic to the public, in a coma. I still visit her everyday around noon. I read to her, talk to her, tell her my dreams, my aspirations. I still think she's going to sit up and come out of it. I no longer want the looks of pity, the kind words of my wife; I want to be free. I want to feel like I can move on without feeling so damn guilty about living my life. I want to live. What do you think I should do? I love my wife, but I hate what she did to me, to us. I want to move on, but

I'm afraid of what her parents will think. I'm afraid of what the person that I care about most will think if I did this.

What would you do if you had someone that cared for you, but was in this situation? Could you see past the pain, the hurt of this man's life, or could you not get over the disgust of being with someone whose wife was in the other room, biding time until she went to the angels?

Confused in Connecticut

Dear Confused,

I can't imagine the way you feel, the way your life had been ripped from you. People can be crude sometimes; they think awful things, but in your situation, being human is the only way that you're going to survive through the hurt, and the pain.

Don't look at it as pity, as judging; look at it as love. This is not your fault. She did this to you. You know what you would've done if she had told you the news.

When people are about to do something like suicide, they aren't in their right mind and cannot see reason through madness. She wanted your child so badly that she couldn't see past the horror of not being able to. Please don't forget the wonderful times that you had together. Don't have hatred towards her; after all, we are only human. Think about the good times you had together and let those times get you through the next eighteen years of your life. Think about living. Your life is the only thing you have that is so precious to you, and you need to take care of it. Embrace it. As far as loving and learning to love again, you have it in you. Don't close

yourself off so this new woman that you love in your life can't see it. Sarah wouldn't want that. She wouldn't want you to suffer the rest of your life like the way she suffered minutes before she ended hers. Move on, take it slowly, and enjoy the ride. She must be a very special person for someone like you to have fallen in love with her. Please keep in touch with me. I would like to see how your story ends, or in this case begins.

Katherine E. Daniels, Freelance

She looked up from the paper at her father smiling from ear-to-ear. "Great advice, Katherine. Warren will be relieved and feel much better."

"Did you know he sent this letter to me? How long have you been plotting? And," she huffed, "why did you make up a story like a surgery to get me to come here?" Her hands went to her hips as she glared at him, the newspaper was now clenched tightly in her fists.

"Kat, don't yell at me, I'm still your father. Besides, he's the right man for you. I was only looking out for your best interests."

"I am thirty-eight years old! When do I get to look out for my own interests? You didn't have to lie to me about a surgery! You could have just asked me to come down."

"Kitten, I know I should've been honest with you, but in the past few years you haven't been exactly forthcoming with your mother and me. You never talk about your relationships with us, your place in New York is the size of the hall closet, and you barely even call us anymore."

She was fuming now, "I don't have to call you because you call every five minutes!"

Bill inhaled then spoke, "Think about it, you wouldn't have come, would you?"

She thought about it and decided that she probably wouldn't have. She liked where she was in her life didn't she? She liked her career. Well, *had* liked was definitely the correct term. She made something of herself in New York. Here in Connecticut, she was still that shy little girl with braces; that awkward teenager that never had a date, or the one with the freakish gang of brothers and gorgeous to die for sister. In New York, she was a woman. She may not have dated much, or at all until a week ago, but she was just fine. *Keep telling yourself that,* she thought. "I... You're probably right. But I'm still mad at you!" A smile started to bubble from the surface as she went over to her father. "I'm sorry; I didn't realize that I've been that bad of a daughter. Warren was right."

Her father cocked his head back a little, "*Warren* was right?"

"The other day, just before this whole mess happened, he told me more or less that I was selfish and I didn't seem to care about you or Mom. I, of course, care about you, but have been selfish. I haven't been the best person to be around lately if ever."

"He said that to you?" Her father looked like he was starting to get angry.

"Yes, but he immediately apologized for that. Then he started in on Kelsey and that whole mess, and by the way I'm still mad about that, so drop it."

Her father smirked. "Well, I still think that guy deserves

a good swift kick, but I can't believe Warren would say something like that. He's such a nice young man. I think you've really gotten to him."

"You say that, but I've only known him for not even a week. And three days of that I haven't even seen him. I'm sorry, but this kind of behavior isn't really a turn on, not to mention him not telling me about his wife."

"He feels like he feels; He probably knows you more than you think he does, and he certainly is a better catch than Kelsey," Bill scoffed. "And, the mention of his wife, she hasn't been in the picture for five years now. I don't think you can really count that as a marriage. Besides, he and I get along, and you know how hard that is for me to like someone that you date."

"We're not dating! You're so delusional! Besides, I'm not into arranged marriages. What *are* you doing? He's going through something that neither of us can even fathom, and here you are acting like it's just a little bump in the road. I'm not going to be the one to pick up all the pieces when he finally falls apart! I'm going back to New York next week!"

Ignoring her last remark he kept on, "I've been meaning to talk to you about that. Do you really think it's a good idea? They obviously don't have any respect for you at that… magazine! Connecticut has so much more to offer you. Why, the Herald is hiring."

"Oh, here we go."

"Don't you 'here we go' me. You… oh, forget it! When you're ready to start acting like an adult…" He stormed off, mumbling things along the way, acting like he was put off by their conversation, then slammed the screen door to the porch.

Shaking her head, she started to talk to herself, "The Herald? You have got to be kidding me! Ha!" She looked at the paper that was clenched tightly in her fist and unfolded it. "What does he know?" The New York Times was what she wanted, at least that's what she kept telling herself.

***

The black SUV pulled in a little after midnight. She was sitting down by herself in front of the pond, having a glass of wine and soaking her feet in the water. The water looked like broken glass as she swayed her feet back and forth. She could never go to bed at a decent hour. It didn't matter how tired she was right now, her mind was running races around New York, what her father said, and about Warren's wife, Sarah.

She heard voices in the distance and wondered why her parents were up at this hour. Probably arguing over he father's bad habit of the midnight snack or what on earth she was doing drinking down at the pond. Then she heard a sound behind her. When she turned to look, Warren sat down, cross-legged on the dock beside her.

"I'm so glad you're up." He smiled tight-lipped.

"Warren."

"Please, don't. You needn't say anything. I feel awful about everything except for this." He pulled the NY Times column from his pocket. He'd folded it several times and slipped it into his wallet.

"Oh, you saw it? Well, I want you to know I would've tried to get it pulled; I just figured out that it was you. I wish you would've told me." She took a drink of her wine and placed the glass back down, swaying her feet in circles in the water.

"Katherine, I know I should've told you. I didn't know how to come out with it. I thought about it several times, the night that you were here. When I met you at the airport you looked so beautiful, and honestly I didn't want to ruin anything. I want to be honest with you, about everything. Hippa laws or not, your father doesn't have a surgery scheduled. I don't know why the hell he would tell you that. Crazy old man!" He smirked when he said it, then looked up at Katherine. "I really like your father."

"I know." She smiled reassuringly. "He likes you, too."

"Anyway, I never planned on any of this happening. I want you to know that. I've been talking to your father for months about you. He's shown me pictures before, of course, and I thought, damn she's beautiful. I never gave it a second thought; I was married.

Then he showed me your column. He started talking about you nearly every day. We'd go fishing and he would bring you up. Instantly, I was curious. I started reading your column, loved your words. I thought, here is a woman that knows how to write, communicate with her readers. And nearly every time I read your column, I agreed with your advice. Sometimes I stood after reading it, cheering you on, saying, damn, right on the money! Then I was hooked. I bought the subscription, turned to the table of contents and found where your column was and read yours first. The rest of the magazine is shit, though." He smiled.

Katherine returned the smile and laughed.

"I loved your words, your face; your beautiful face was

just a bonus. Then your father started telling me things like what you like to do and the places that you go to. He showed me a picture of your place in New York, things like that. I felt like I've known you for years. I stopped going to the hospital as much, then just looked forward to reading your column. I talked to your father, and he told me that you usually come home for Christmas. I'd been planning my vacation around meeting you.

Then this past month I had a few rough times, thinking of Sarah, feeling guilty about my feelings for you—someone I'd never even met. I talked to your father about it. He told me that I should take a vacation, try to sort things out. He suggested I write to your column, see what you think. I can't believe the New York Times printed this." He held up the article in his hand and shook his head.

"Then your father told me a week ago that your sister was going to pick you up at the airport. I was so excited that I offered to drive. When I saw you, I knew that I had to get to know you better. I'm sorry if I scared you, if you're disgusted by me. I don't know, I can't explain it. Then *my* Sarah died."

She looked at his face when he mentioned her name. "I'm so sorry, Warren. My mother told me what happened. And, so did you, of course. In a way, you did tell me," she said shyly.

Warren gave her a closed mouth smile. "I guess I did." He looked at her and grabbed her hand; she didn't move she just listened to him. "It felt like my whole world came crashing down. I'd finally moved on, thinking I may have a chance with someone, to move on, then as I was holding you, and God it was wonderful, she died." He swallowed hard.

She sat there, listening to him, holding his hand, and thinking of the right thing to say to him in response to what he had just said. When she opened her mouth to speak, she went blank. He was almost professing his love to her. This man whom, days ago, she decided would be fun to have a little affair with, then go back to New York in better shape. She now knew what a huge mistake that would have been. "Warren, I really don't know what to say, I feel awful about Sarah. I feel in my heart, though, that I gave you the right advice about her, but I feel dumb for saying this... the other woman you speak of, is that me?"

"Yes," he said as he uncrossed his legs and put them in the water beside hers.

"But you don't even know me. I know you say you do, but that is just what my father told you. You can't possibly have feelings for me?"

He felt mildly stupid to say the least. How could he feel that way? "I don't know, I just do. I don't know; it isn't really a good answer, is it? God, when I kissed you here. Our first kiss—I felt something, almost like..."

"Electricity," she said, starting out at the pond.

"Yes, I knew you had to feel it, too." He smiled faintly as he thought of the moment when the boat moved and she fell into his eager arms.

"I did." She was thinking of that night, also.

He wished he could kiss her right now, but didn't want to scare her away. He didn't know what she thought of him. If she thought he was a jerk for making a move days after his wife passed, when in reality Sarah had been gone for the last five years. Just realizing it himself he felt a little lighter, less depressed about being here with her.

"Can we start over? I know it's a little lame, but I feel something with you that I haven't felt in a long time. And I mean, a long time."

She looked over at his soft eyes—eyes that held such conviction, such warmth. She wanted to say no, and knew she should with everything that she had, but couldn't. "Maybe."

"I will take that," he said. He pulled his legs out of the water and faced her. He smiled then introduced himself. "Hi, I'm Warren Vance. It's a pleasure to have finally met you."

She let out a little giggle. "The pleasure has been all mine."

CHAPTER SEVEN

The smell of Starbucks coffee brewing in the coffeemaker made its way through the hallway to her bedroom. She almost felt like she was in New York again, minus the sounds of ambulances and police cars zooming around throughout the night. She sat on the edge of her bed and stretched her arms out wide. Deciding it was going to be a great morning, she placed her fuzzy red slippers on her feet and walked out into the kitchen with nothing but her nightshirt and panties on. Her sister was having a small dispute with her brother, Kyle. They were arguing over whose show they were going to watch. "Aren't you both a little old for that?" She grinned and pulled a small red mug from the cupboard overhead, then grabbed the coffee pot and poured a warm cup.

"Don't forget, sis, you tower us by age!" Kyle smart-mouthed back. Smiling, he nudged his other sister in the side.

"I can't help it if you were all accidents!"

They all laughed as their mother and father walked into the kitchen. "Still at it I see. We're going to have to separate you into the corners like old times," Gail said as she smiled at Katherine, Kyle and Karen. Katherine walked to the door.

"Like always, it was Karen and Kyle. I'm innocent in all of this," Katherine said.

"Of course, my Katherine would never do anything like that," Bill said, tousling his eldest's hair. Kyle and Karen scoffed as Katherine stuck her tongue out in protest.

"Hey, your boyfriend's here, Kat," Kyle joked.

Katherine looked out the window. "Very funny, Kyle. Surprised you never got a job in a comedy club."

"I know; me, too," Kyle said, thoughtfully looking up in a dramatic way. "I'm quite the thespian."

Katherine laughed as she walked to the door. Forgetting that she was barely clothed and her hair was tangled up into a haphazard ponytail, she waved at him and smiled. He got out of his truck, and came towards her.

Noticing the fuzzy red slippers, he grinned. "I have to get me a pair of those. They look exceedingly comfortable."

"Oh, my God!" She looked down, noticed her feet. Then her hands went to her head and patted her hair, as it donned on her what she must have looked like. She could only imagine her teeth at this point. Realizing her legs were bare and she was wearing a black t-shirt with "Got Milk" printed on the front, she was mortified! It was like her worst nightmare coming to life. Her face must have painted what she was thinking all over it. He started laughing as she excused herself to the bathroom, slamming the door in his face. He laughed as he pushed the door open.

"Good morning, Bill. Ready?"

"Warren! Good morning! You want something to eat? I'm thinking of a slice of heart attack and a side of heart burn!" Gail rolled her eyes in disgust as she opened the refrigerator, pulling out the bacon and eggs.

"You should be following the diet plan that I laid out for you, Bill," Warren said just above a whisper so Gail wouldn't hear.

Bill nodded his head as Gail spoke, "Are you hungry,

108

Warren?"

"Thanks, Gail, if it's no trouble."

"None at all, you sit down and get comfortable. Everything going well? How are your parents doing?" Gail asked as she broke the eggs into the skillet.

"Everything is much better, thank you. Mom and Dad are getting ready to go back to Georgia as we speak. I drove them to the airport an hour ago."

"Glad to hear it. Plans for today?" Bill ventured.

Warren glanced at him suspiciously. "No, just fishing with you."

"About the fishing, you're going out, but not with us. We're going to the movies; aren't we, Gail?" Bill said, wriggling his eyebrows up and down.

"Oh, Bill!" Gail laughed.

"God, Dad, do you have to talk like that?" Karen asked.

"We aren't dead yet, baby. Hey, you never know, you might have a new brother or sister soon." Bill laughed.

Kyle looked into the kitchen now. "That's just gross. You guys can't possibly still..."

"Every night, unless it's a full moon, and then we do it twice." Bill winked, then stood up and smacked his wife on the butt. Gail rolled her eyes and Karen made a gag motion with her finger up to her mouth.

Warren sat at the table, struggling to eat his bacon and eggs. He loved this family. "Well, we don't want to be here when she gets out, so we'll get out of your hair. Remember, be nice," Bill said.

"I will. Thank you for breakfast, Gail. Bill, as always, you're nuts." Bill smiled as he quickly ushered his family out of the house.

After a quick shower and a makeup lesson, Kat pulled herself together quite well. Minus the "Got Milk" disaster and her fuzzy teeth, she was eager to take on the world. Well, at least the coffee that she left in the kitchen. She pulled her hair back into a ponytail and dressed in her Calvin Klein boot cut jeans and a black v-neck t-shirt. She wore a single gold chain around her neck and hoop earrings in her ears. She looked good, much better; maybe a little too obvious for her parents, but who cares. She walked out into the kitchen and everyone had gone. She smelled the traces of breakfast and noticed a solitary plate on the table with some bacon and scrambled eggs on it.

When she sat down, she heard the front door open. Just as the fork reached her mouth, Warren came around the corner holding the mail. He handed her some letters as he sat down appraising her. "You look great."

She blushed slightly. "Thank you, and thanks for getting mail. Is everyone outside?"

"Ah, no. They left. Your dad said something about a noon movie at Cinema Ten. They told me it was theater nine if we want to join them."

"Warren, if you wanted to go, you should have. I've got some work to do today." Actually, this was a lie, but he didn't know about her career mishap. She had to speak with her lawyer about the lawsuit, and better yet, she had to find out if anyone called about the newest job opening for the Times.

"I thought we could take a walk today, maybe catch a movie, later, after dinner of course." He smiled at her as she put down her fork.

"I don't know."

"Come on. You have to eat, don't you? You won't be disappointed." He batted his eyes a little and laid a big grin on her. She smiled back and picked her fork up.

"Okay, you got me. Where do you want to walk?"

"I was thinking maybe downtown. Maybe we can go to the bookstore, and cookie shop, and then back to my house. I thought I could cook for you."

"Wow, you cook, too? Well, I guess I will have to take you up on that, but I will help."

"Sounds good."

She finished her breakfast and washed the dishes. When she finished, she pulled out a pair of black cowboy boots. She received them last Christmas and left them in the closet here at her parents. She never wore boots in New York, knee high boots, but *country* wasn't exactly New York's style. Warren was dressed in Levis and a black button down shirt. He looked great, too.

She decided it was great walking beside him. Many women on the street passed them and turned their heads, checking out his fine behind. She could've been jealous, but instead felt like he was a trophy that she could carry around. They walked into a few shops, making small talk along the way. They stopped into a small bookstore and talked about their favorite authors and books. They both liked poetry. *Emerson* was her favorite and *Frost* was his. They both had a love for *Stephen King*, and his *Dead Zone* series. Authors like *Terry Goodkind, J.K. Rowling,* and *Lee Duncan* were a few that kept coming to mind when she thought about her favorite Fantasy novels. When she talked about how much she liked the book, *IRIS: A*

Dragon's Perspective, Warren saw passion in her eyes. He took a mental picture of that look, cataloguing it in his thoughts for later. He thought that she was much like the heroine, *Xandria Shaw,* with her tough exterior and exquisite beauty.

Throughout the trip, they found that they had much in common: books, movies, theater. They quoted many famous lines from the different films that they've seen, making a game of it during their day of endless shopping and gadding.

They had a small lunch of egg rolls and rice at the *House of Hunan* on the corner of Third and Wallace. "Well, do you want to head back to my house soon? I'm thinking dancing...then dinner, then movie?" He smiled at her. She thought he could destroy her with that one look.

"Yes, sounds perfect." He took her hand in his and led the way to Fifth and Rosedale. They made it there within a half hour. They were certainly working off their calories for the day. Warren talked about how he is used to walking. Frequently, he just walked to his office from his house so he had the time to blow off steam, to think. She thought that was a good idea. She walked ninety percent of the time in New York.

They entered the house and she noticed all of the flowers that were meticulously placed. She felt a little awkward being in the home with all of his wife's flowers.

"I'm sorry about all the flowers; I realize it may make you uncomfortable." He shifted his weight onto his right side as he leaned against the counter. "You want to go downstairs?"

She nodded and smiled softly. He took her hand as

they walked through the basement door and she noticed right away that it was like the man cave her brothers always wanted. There were shelves lining the one wall with an assortment of leather bound books, brand new books and old ones with the covers slightly torn. In the center of the short wall, was a mantle with a fireplace and on the wall to her left was a huge sectional couch with a cherry coffee table in front of it. The area was beautiful; very homey, very much Warren.

"I love this room! My brothers would love this! The books are great. My apartment looks much the same with the shelves and all of the books. The couch has to be my favorite part, though."

Warren smiled from ear-to-ear, "I bought that couch a little over a year ago; always wanted one."

"A couch? Don't set your sights too high, do you?" She laughed.

He looked at her and grinned. God how he loved her laugh; it was almost musical.

"Well, I guess not. Sarah wouldn't let me get a sectional couch. She thought they were a bit tacky for her taste. So, I never gave it much thought, then last year when I was walking by Stanton's, I bought it. It may be tacky, but it is damn comfortable, and besides, this area here is all mine, and she had nothing to do with it." Warren smiled, then immediately frowned, feeling bad about the last part.

"I'm sorry," she said.

"Don't be. It's true. I've let things bother me for way too long. Don't think of me as broken, please."

"I don't, it's just…"

"Don't worry about anything. You're perfect. You couldn't say anything that I haven't already heard a thousand times. I'm so glad that you're here with me. I had a great time today."

"Me, too."

Warren walked over to the small *Bose* stereo sitting above the fireplace and switched on a CD. He held out his hand and she took it.

"Dance with me?" Kat nodded, then he pulled her into his warm embrace. With his hand at the small of her back, he led her across the room gracefully.

He could dance. He smelled great, too. His hair looked just as delicious as he smelled; she wanted to run her fingers through it. Finally, a man that could not only dance, but was very easy on the eyes.

As he twirled her around the room to Frank Sinatra, he genuinely felt happy for the first time in a long time. "Thank you," he said then pulled her into a hug. She fit perfectly into his body; he couldn't help but think of her in his bed. "Would you like something to drink?" he asked.

"Yes, thank you. It's a little hot in here, isn't it? Do you have the air on?" She pulled at the neckline of her t-shirt then followed him up the stairs to the kitchen.

"Water, wine or soda?"

"Water is just fine," she said. He handed her a bottle of natural spring water. She took the cap off and downed its contents in a couple of gulps.

Warren stifled back a laugh as he watched her.

She put the bottle on the counter. "I didn't realize how thirsty I was."

"Would you like more?" He cocked his eyebrow up.

She could never understand how that one gesture could do so much for a situation. It had so many different meanings. She had to laugh.

"No, it's okay."

"Alright, well this is a bit awkward, isn't it?" *Sure it is... all you've been thinking about is how she would feel in your arms, in your bed, how making love to her would feel so wonderful, how long it's been for you...*

"A little, sorry."

"Please don't apologize. You're going to have to start paying the toll if you apologize to me again." He gestured to his lips, "Right here with a little kiss the next time you say you're sorry. Come on, I dare you."

He was being cute. She was relieved that he knew how to remedy her nervousness. She could think of a few things to fix that. She was attracted to him, heaven help her. Standing in a close proximity with a man like Warren Vance could only mean one thing...trouble. And all she wanted to do was flirt. "Now, I will really make sure that I don't."

"We'll see about that. I'm pretty good at having women apologize."

"Really?" Now it was her turn for the eyebrow.

"No, but I've had *great* practice with you." He laughed a belly laugh at her expression, then turned to the refrigerator. "Ah, there is some great stuff in here. Now, is there anything at all that you're allergic to before I start the feast?"

"I'm surprised my father didn't give you a list of my medical history. I'm shocked," she said while pretending to fan herself.

"Funny, funny, Katherine. Are you going to keep giving me shit about that? Because if you are, this isn't going to work."

She looked at him; she didn't know if he was joking or not. "Sorry, maybe this was a bad idea!" she said as she turned for the door. Her face reddened as she grabbed the doorknob.

"Gotcha!" he said as his left forefinger gave the come-hither signal and pressed a finger to his lips. "Man, this is going to be much easier than I thought!"

She walked over, half a mind to slap him, then saw his wide grin. "You suck!" She smiled as she went to kiss his cheek, then he pulled her into him.

"You know, I can stand like this all day with you." She moaned softly, and smiled; the same one that he first saw when she got off the airplane. He bent his head down, "I'm going to kiss you—now," he said quietly.

She knew it even before he said it, as his eyes darkened and he bent his head down so his lips could brush hers. "Good." *What was she saying? This was way too fast with her. A week ago she was hoping to use him, have sex, then go back to New York. This was turning into a relationship. Oh, God…a relationship in Connecticut.* She didn't even want to think of it. She stopped the kiss. His face sulked.

"You okay? Where were you just now?"

"I think we're moving a bit too fast… I don't want to be the rebound girl." *Rebound girl? Really, where was the duct tape when she needed it?*

He let go of her gently and walked over to the sink. He grabbed a washcloth and started to wash some dishes in

116

the sink. He didn't say anything for a few minutes which made the situation all the more awkward, then he turned around. "You know," his voice was a little bit louder, angrier. "I haven't so much as looked at another woman for five God damn years!"

She could see that he needed to get this out, so she didn't say anything.

"FIVE YEARS!" he threw his hands up in the air as he looked at her. His eyes were battling an inner war. "I haven't touched a woman, thought of a woman, looked at a woman, nothing. FIVE YEARS! This shit has taken me down. Five years I've felt guilty about Sarah sitting in that hospital room, five years I watched her from a chair, thinking that we would be together, that she would wake up and walk out of that hospital. I was delusional thinking that I'd even want her after what she did." He was angry, angry with himself for the way he was talking. He shook his head, ran his fingers through his hair, and paced nervously.

Katherine looked at him, tears threatened to escape her eyes. "I'm so sorry, Warren. I didn't mean to..."

"That's two, Kat." Then he turned the conversation back. "I can't believe how my world has been rocked by this woman. She finds out something that we should have both worked through. She leaves it up to herself, then decides that she can't handle it. Now I'm left for the past five fucking years sulking in a corner; probably now really unable to have children with someone. She has done this not only to herself, but also to me all over again. Then when I finally start to clear this out of my mind; the guilt, the racking pain, you think I'm using you in some sort of cat and mouse game, excuse the expression..."

"That's not what..."

"It's exactly what you meant. Damn it, Kat, don't you see how special you are to me? You have no idea how much you've gotten me through this past year: your column, your picture, you. I know this sounds a bit off, but when you came here, I felt my world get a little lighter. I can see us together, with a future, see me with a future. It makes me happy as hell. You look so damn good in this place with me. You feel great in my arms, and I can only imagine what it feels like to..." He stopped, feeling flustered, his face reddened as he watched her take in what he had just said. "Hell." He walked over to her, grabbed her arm tightly and pushed her against the dishwasher. "I'm taking what's mine, and you, girl, owe me two."

Her eyes widened in shock and passion as he put his hands up to her face and tilted her neck back; pressing kisses down her neck. He could feel the pulse of her heart and its rhythm against him. Her breathing became heavy, as he ran his finger down, feeling her nice, taut skin. Then he trailed his mouth back toward hers, lingering a while on her ear, sucking at her earlobe, then to her lips. Her nice full bottom lip was begging to be taken. He bit her softly, after he heard a small moan escape her parted lips, and it only made him want her more. He took her in further, tasting her, indulging himself in the kiss.

She kissed him back with the same intensity. Her arms floated down to his sides as she felt his hard body press against her own. She pulled them up his back feeling the muscles tighten as she ran her nails down his shirt. He slowly moved his hands to her hips and lifted her gently off the floor, placing her on the counter behind her. Her breast heaved as she inhaled; her eyes looked at him in passion as she bit on her bottom lip.

He had to have her. His hands moved up her legs to her hips, then to the bottom of her shirt where he slowly lifted it to expose her black, lacy bra. He groaned as his fingers traced the top of her arms where the straps to her bra were. He gently slid them down, exposing her shoulder. He brushed kisses down her shoulder then around her neck to the top of her breasts. He reached around with his hands and unclasped the bra. She let her arms fall as the bra slipped from its place, exposing her breasts.

Immediately, he gave them the attention they deserved.

She had perfect nipples, the color of coral. He took one in his mouth, teasing it with his tongue while he touched the other lightly with his other hand. She moaned and moved her hands through his hair.

"I want you," she said huskily.

"God, I want you, Katherine," he said as his breath became more ragged. His hands went to her beltline; slowly undid the button and slid the zipper down. Her hand went down upon his. He stopped what he was doing. She must've wanted to stop. When he backed away, he saw her undoing the snap herself. He exhaled, and thanked God that she didn't want to stop, then took her into his arms and carried her into his bedroom.

The bedroom was large with a sleigh bed caddy-corner

on one wall with a fireplace on the other. Dark hardwood floors made the white rug stand out. The walls were a calming pale blue with wispy, white curtains donning the windows. He gently laid her on the bed, then slowly took off her jeans.

Her legs were gorgeous, long and muscular. Her eyes were closed as she arched her back. He crawled between her thighs and reached for her panties with his teeth.

She could feel him on her skin, her breathing was ragged; her pulse was so fast she didn't know if she could stand the wait much longer. She pulled him over her with his belt and began kissing him some more. Her hands found the strength to undo the zipper of his pants and, with his help, pulled them off.

"I want this to be perfect," Warren whispered, looking to her. He turned and pulled a match from the night table and lit a candle that sat on top of it, then went back to kissing her.

She smiled inwardly. This man was something out of her dreams.

His hands fell down to her hips, gently stroking her making their way to her inner thigh. Her body trembled at his touch. Softly, he brushed his fingers against her core. Warm liquid heat threatened to erupt from her as he touched her gently. She wanted him; she needed him inside of her. "Now, please, now." She didn't think she could take anymore teasing. The way he looked was more than enough for her; he went to the dresser for protection, sheathed himself then slid back into position, pulling himself up to her.

He went inside, slowly. She rocked her hips back and

forth as he felt the warmth of her explode onto him, shivers went down his spine as he moved to her rhythm, and she gasped as he sped up, moving faster until finally the ramifications of his passion were released. She felt him fill her, she felt his heartbeat, and she felt his lips on hers as they made love.

***

The streets weren't paved with gold like she imagined, but they weren't filled with smog or dirt either. She was back in the void. She'd been here before. The last time, she had had a job to do; she was supposed to bring two people together, and she was damn proud of the job she did. Only she had to resort to the same outcome as before. She shook her head at the irony.

She tried a few different times to bring them together. Nothing worked. Although it was her responsibility, she loved her husband deeply. She didn't want to give him up. Once she met him, she knew she'd gone and done it. She fell in love with him. She didn't want the other woman to have him.

In her heart of hearts, she knew that he was meant for her and she was meant for him, like God said the last time, it was destiny. *Ah the hell with destiny*, but when she found out she couldn't get pregnant, she knew it was God's way of telling her it wasn't meant to be. She wasn't meant for him. Then miraculously, she remembered why she was there in the first place and took the steps to end her life and start Warren's with Katherine.

"You know I'm not happy with what you've done, Sarah," the deep voice said, suddenly emerging from the lighted staircase, appearing from the dark void of the room.

"Oh, I did what you wanted, didn't I?" she said, annoyed.

"No, you didn't. You were supposed to put them together; you weren't supposed to end your life to do it. And, you were never supposed to hurt him. You nearly killed him, too."

God was angry. She'd never seen him like this. Sure, she'd seen Him mad before but not disappointed in her; that was a different feeling all together. When God was disappointed with you, it meant something.

"I'm sorry. I know what I was supposed to do. I got caught up with the life down there. I never had a baby; I really wanted one, and you presented me with a wonderful man. Before I knew it, I wanted him just as badly as Katherine does now."

"That's beside the point, Sarah. When you ask of things up here, you may get it. You weren't supposed to defy me like that," He said strongly.

"I'm sorry, you know I am. I don't like what I did to him. But, I can honestly say, it helped bring her to him. She will love him completely, even more now."

"I hope you're right," He said, shaking his head now, looking at the pictures that filled the void. "They do look happy, don't they?"

She looked at the couple that was in each other's arms, "Yes, they do. He loves her, and I know she loves him."

God nodded. "Come on, Sarah, your family is waiting." She smiled. It had been a long time since she had seen them. Tears spilled from her eyes.

"Thank you, so much."

"You're welcome," He said. They both looked down at the couple once more before gliding up the golden stairway.

***

The mess of legs and tangled sheets left little to the imagination as the upper half of Katherine was exposed. Warren lay beside her, staring down at her body in his. His finger ran slight shivers down her spine as she awoke to him, touching her and feasting with his eyes. "Hi," she said dreamily.

"Hi, yourself," he said, looking at her mouth. "You have a great mouth." He brushed his lips against hers and kissed her again.

"Mmm, thank you." She reddened slightly, then pulled the sheet up to cover herself.

He pulled the sheet down to where it was. "Now why ruin a perfect moment?" He smiled at her eyes as they rounded in surprise, "You're so beautiful."

She felt beautiful. Making love with Warren felt so delicious. She was relaxed, yet nervous at the same time, excited at the prospect of this man making love to her again. He was perfect; his skin, his body, his smile, his laugh. *Oh, God she was falling in love with him.*

"What are you thinking about?" he mused.

"What? Nothing..."

"Yes, you are. When you're thinking about something, your cute little nose scrunches up." He smiled as he kissed her nose, then looked right back into her eyes.

"It does?"

"Yes, it does," he said, kissing her again.

"Oh, well, I was thinking about how wonderful I feel."

She said it aloud. Why doesn't she just stamp *I'm falling for you* on her forehead?

"Good, I thought you were going to say something else. Thank God. I feel great. You were wonderful, are wonderful." He brushed her hair behind her ears as he kissed the top of her head.

As awkward as she should feel right now, she felt oddly comfortable. Lying in his arms, in his bed, it felt perfect; too perfect.

"I'm afraid to ask, but are you hungry?"

She laughed a little. "I thought you would never ask!"

They stood in the kitchen where this whole thing started, as he smiled and opened up the refrigerator. He got out the mushrooms, onions, tomatoes, chicken breast, and fresh parmesan. She liked the way he moved in the kitchen. He had a smile on his face, and she was happy to know she put it on there. He pulled a bottle of wine off the rack beside the refrigerator. "Wine, my lady?"

"Sounds good, need some help with dinner?"

"I have this covered. Why don't you go downstairs and relax." She smiled as he took her hand and led her down the stairs. "This couch has your name all over it. Prop your feet up, here's the remote. Help yourself to any of the movies or if you like, the CDs are that cabinet over there." He gestured to a small bureau in the corner.

"A man after my own heart." She sighed dramatically.

"I aim to please," he said then blew a kiss as he walked back up the steps to the kitchen.

Several minutes later, the aromas wafting from the kitchen made her taste buds tickle. She could smell fresh tomatoes, basil, garlic, and if she was right, a hint of rosemary. Pasta was her weakness. She could hear him moving in the kitchen. She sighed as she turned off the television. She watched an old rerun of the *Golden Girls*, deciding she wanted to be more like Blanche Deveroux, sexy and confident. She laughed to herself then picked her wineglass off the coffee table and made her way up the steps.

"Mmm, it smells so good in here, and looks great, too."

"It just got even better," he said and smiled as he pulled out a chair for her. She sat down then he moved her hair to the side to kiss her neck. "This is going to be the death of me." She laughed a throaty laugh, which threatened to crush him. He thought he had better sit down before his knees gave out.

"So, where did you learn to cook? This tastes wonderful." She picked up the fork, twirling her pasta then took a bite. She couldn't help but notice the choice of wine and smiled. He definitely knew how to charm.

"Well, before deciding to be a doctor, I took a few cooking classes at a community college. My father said it was a good idea, how to get the ladies... if I remember correctly."

She laughed. "Nice, good man... that sounds like something Dad would say to my brothers."

"Yes, definitely."

Everything was great, natural. The conversation, the mood, the whole day was looking to be the best in his life. He couldn't stop thinking about making love to her, feeling his body in hers, the way they fit, like two pieces in a puzzle. The...

The phone rang. Warren shook the thoughts off, "Excuse me for a moment." He stood up, wiped his mouth with a napkin then went to the phone. "Hold on, hold on."

"Hello, this is Warren."

"Warren? This is Gail."

"Gail, hi, how're you doing?"

Kat edged off her seat then followed him into the kitchen. She saw the look on Warren's face then stepped back a little.

"Gail, everything's going to be okay, I'll be there. Kat and I will be there in a few minutes. No, don't worry about that. You aren't interrupting anything. Did you call...? Good, you did everything you could; I will be right over." He hung up the phone and grabbed his keys off the hook by the refrigerator. "Katherine, we have to go; that was your mother."

"Is she alright, is dad?"

"It's okay, stay calm. We're going to the hospital. They think your dad may have had another heart attack. But he's in the hospital now, so he'll be just fine."

Katherine started crying, shaking as she stood there, and listening to what he said.

"Come on now, everything is going to be okay. I'm going to make sure of it. I wouldn't let anything happen to that father of yours." He smiled reassuringly then rubbed the tears away from her face.

CHAPTER EIGHT

The trip to the hospital had Kat bundled in nerves. She barely spoke two words since they left his house. "It's going to be okay, Katherine. I'll be there with you." He put his hand on hers and she let their fingers entwine.

"Thank you, I hope so..." She started crying again. Her eyes were swollen from the tears as they pulled into the hospital parking lot. She wiped her eyes with her free hand and braced herself as Warren pulled his keys from the ignition. He got out of the car and walked around to her side, opening the door to help her. He took her hand as they walked into the hospital. Katherine's mom and sister were standing at the counter.

"Oh, I'm so glad that you two are here!" she cried as she crushed them with her arms. "They just took him in. I gave him a kiss before. He told me to tell you both something if," she couldn't stop crying.

"Don't talk like that, Mom! He's going to be just fine." She hoped that was the truth. She knew that Warren would keep his promise. She let go of his hand and took her mother's. "Please don't think that way. Think positive thoughts. What happened?"

"I'm going to go in there and see if there's anything I can do. I don't understand why they didn't page me. I'm his doctor."

"Warren, he requested that they didn't bother you. He wanted you to stay with Kat." She looked up, pierced her lips together in a small smile, then squeezed Katherine's hand.

"Oh, well I'm going in anyway. I'll be back, Katherine, Gail." He kissed the top of Kat's head and gave her mom one last hug before he disappeared into the double swinging doors.

***

"What do you think is taking so long?" Gail Daniels said to her family in the waiting room. "You would think someone could come out and..."

From the double doors, Warren emerged fully dressed in scrubs, pulled his facemask off and looked very tired, but a small smile emerged. "We believe everything is going to be alright. He gave us quite a scare in there, but he pulled through. He's in recovery right now. But, if you want, Gail, you can go in, only for a few minutes. He needs his rest, and you look like you could use something to eat."

"Oh, Warren! Thank you so much!" Gail ran over to him and gave him a big hug and kissed him on the cheek.

"Now you're going to make me blush if you keep doing that! Only a few minutes, five at the most, then I want you boys to get her something to eat." He looked over at her sons and smiled. They all nodded as he walked over to Katherine. "Are you alright?" he whispered softly.

"I... Oh, Warren!" She put her arms around him, and kissed him. "Thank you."

"You're welcome." He kissed her back as everyone watched. Her brothers didn't seem to mind for once, and Karen had a big grin on her face. "I better get back in there. I have some things I still have to check on. He's not out of the woods yet, but he's certainly better than he was."

Katherine nodded and held back the tears. "Thanks."

128

He turned around and made his way through the doors.

***

The whole next week, Katherine had her hands full with her father's complaining.

"Bacon? Come on, Kat... Don't you want your daddy to be happy?" William Daniels cholesterol had hit new records at his last check-up. He wasn't supposed to have anything except dry toast and oatmeal.

"I don't think so. How can you even ask me that? You just had bypass surgery for God sake! You don't get anything unless it is on the list Warren gave me!" She had the same fiery spirit as her old man. They met each other head-to-head. If he thought he was going to get away with things with her, he had another think coming. *Bacon... shit.*

"Speaking of the young doctor, how're you two doing?" With a not so subtle expression on his face, he looked her way.

She rolled her eyes. "What are you talking about? There is nothing going on between..."

The door swung open and Warren stood there with two Styrofoam cups from Starbucks in his hands; his eyes looked sad, he must've heard her.

"Um, Hi, Bill. I thought I would stop by to check on you. How're you doing?" His voice was a bit unsteady as he talked.

"Doing well, Doc. Katherine here is following your directions to a T... won't let me eat a damn thing. Think you could give an old man a break?" Her father glanced towards Katherine and noticed her eyes, then Warren's. "Well, I'm getting a bit tired. I think I'm going to rest; too much excitement for one morning." Bill stood up and went straight towards the bedroom. Katherine rolled her eyes.

"I better get going, too. I have some things to do at the office, at home, I have to go." He fiddled for the keys in his pocket then opened the door.

Katherine looked at him as he left. She didn't know what to do. Sure she had the best sex of her life a few days ago with him. She thought of him constantly, she was so glad to see him come through that door that her heart threatened to burst, but she couldn't go after him. She needed to think. She needed to go back to New York; she needed her old life back.

Bill Daniels turned around to his eldest daughter and gave her the "what for" look. "You know you better go out there! You're going to ruin everything!"

"What are you talking about? Ruin, everything? You're so dramatic!"

"Who's talking? You know he must have heard you! Now get your skinny ass out there and apologize."

"I will do no such thing. There isn't anything—"

"Going on between you? Now, Kat, how stupid do I look? Your mother told me that you came into the hospital holding hands that night. You were at his house! Your brothers told me that you kissed him in the waiting room, and now you're telling me nothing's going on? That's a whole lot of nothing!"

"I..." She put her hands up to her head. "It's none of your business. Here you are meddling with my life again!" she yelled.

Warren could hear their voices coming from the outside. He listened for a while then opened his car door.

"You're making an ass of yourself, Katherine. Can't you tell that the man is taken with you?"

"Understatement of the year, Dad. Whose fault is that? There's one problem though, as much as I would love to have something with him, he lives here! I live in New York! How in the hell do you think that's going to work?" She yelled one last time, rolling her eyes. The door opened abruptly, Warren looked unhinged. Katherine's shoulders fell, and she closed her eyes.

"Listen here, Katherine, Bill. You," he gestured his hand to Bill, "Need not to get excited! You just had a fucking heart attack! And, *you*," he said as he looked at Kat menacingly, "Need not to get him all riled up! Do I need to camp out here, so you can both grow up a bit? Stop this shit!"

Bill's eyes grew wide then held back a smile. "Don't talk that way in front of my daughter!"

"Oh, forget it! This whole family is *nuts*! I think that one minute I may have some... forget it!" He threw his arms up, noticing the wild look in Katherine's eyes then turned on his heel and went out the door. "Call me if you need me!" he yelled from the driveway.

Bill Daniels had many expressions that he used on a daily basis, but by the look on his face and the laugh that escaped his mouth, Kat couldn't determine which one it was. "That boy has got it bad! And so do you."

Katherine shook her head and huffed. All she could do is think of her place in New York and how it wouldn't work, and how she wished it would. "I leave in a few days; I can't get mixed up in your little fantasy." Then she turned and went into the bedroom, slamming her door.

***

Gail Daniels came home from work that night exhausted. Cooking at *Zorans* was the highlight of her life most nights, but tonight she pulled a fourteen hour shift, with hardly any help at all. Her Sous Chef called off and then her backup decided not to show.

It was nearly ten o'clock when she got home. She rolled her neck back and stretched her shoulders as she walked in the door. Katherine was at the sink.

"Hi, Mom. Wow, it's late," she said, looking at the clock. "Are you working like this a lot?"

"Hi, baby. Occasionally this happens. Mostly I'm there in the mornings, doing prep work and the management end. Tonight was just awful, Martin, my Sous-Chef, didn't show up, and then when my shift was over, Chef Lauren didn't show." She shook her head in disgust, then looked up at her daughter. "How's your father?"

"He's fine. Stubborn as hell! He kept trying to get me to feed him things off the list."

Gail giggled to herself; she knew how Bill could be. She'd been his wife for fifty-five years; he was a rascal. "Well, I'm glad you're here. I don't know if I could've resisted that charm of his." She smiled as she took her coat off and hung it on the hook beside the door.

"Charm?" Kat rolled her eyes, never once did she know Bill Daniels to have *charm*.

"Well, there was none of that."

"What's got you all up in arms?" her mother rounded on her as she opened the refrigerator, pulling out a two liter of *Coke*. Katherine opened her mouth to speak when her father came into view.

132

"Lover's spat," came his surly voice. "She and Warren are in that *stage*, and she doesn't want to admit it." He made a dramatic sigh and put his hand over his heart crossing it. Gail's eyes twinkled as she held back a laugh.

"Oh, Bill, honestly!" she said, then put her arms around him. "I've missed you."

"Not as much as I missed you, Gaily."

Katherine, ignoring their love professions, began, "We are not... I don't have to justify myself to anyone! I'm leaving in a few days. Mom, can you get it into his thick skull that this won't work?"

"Oh, Katherine, I don't think so. You see, I think there's something between you two. You and Warren," she said dreamily.

"Oh, God, not you, too."

"The way he held you in the hospital and kissed your forehead almost made me swoon," she said, laughing as Bill nudged her. Katherine rolled her eyes again.

"I have to get some work done, when cupid leaves... let me know. I need a ride into town tomorrow; I have a prescription to fill."

Bill's eyes lit up as she left the room. "You thinking what I'm thinking?"

Gail turned to her husband and kissed his lips. "I'll get the phone!"

Warren lay down on his bed thinking of the first night he spent with Kat. He brought the pillow up to his face and inhaled her scent. He could still smell her there; feel her in his bed. Why was she doing this to him? He knew that she was going back to New York, but he thought that maybe she'd want to be home, liked being home.

He was wrong. He'd heard what she said. If that was going to be his only night with her he wouldn't spoil it by stewing in his room. When he woke up, he'd have to find another way to convince her to be with him. Imagining her in his arms, he smiled and fell asleep.

Ten minutes later the phone rang, and he groaned then reached over to the side table and picked it up, "Hello?"

"Warren," Bill Daniel's voice called.

God, he couldn't get a minute's rest from this family. If he wasn't thinking about them, they were calling. "No, I'm actually in bed, are you alright?"

"Oh, sorry, son. You were sleeping? It's only eleven. Wow...you need a hobby."

"Bill, is everything alright?" Warren asked shortly.

"Sorry, Warren, I just... well, Kat needs to go to the pharmacy in the morning, and I was thinking if you weren't doing anything you could take her. Gail's been pulling doubles, and I need my rest." Gail smiled and leaned into the receiver, listening.

"No, sorry, Bill. As much as I would love to help her out... you out... I can't. I have to go. You call me if you need anything, medically. Goodnight." His voice sounded broken. Gail shook her head and put her hand up to her mouth.

"Oh, sorry, son. I hope everything's okay. Gail and I will be thinking of you. Give us a call later and let us know how you're doing." He looked to Gail with an odd expression on his face.

The line went dead. Bill turned to Gail, "The boy

worries me, I'm going to go over there and talk to him."

"You can't do that, Bill. You can't fix everything. Let him mull it over for a while, then if we don't hear from him in a few days, you can go over."

"You're right, Gaily...You're right." He smiled to his wife and gave her a kiss. "Let's do some kissing," Bill said affectionately as he led his wife to the bedroom. "Doesn't that sound good?"

"Sure does."

***

Katherine sat in her room finishing the paperwork her lawyer sent to her. In a few days she would have enough money to live for a few years without a job. She smiled thinking about all the things she could get with it for her apartment. She needed a new computer, no scratch that, she wanted a new computer. She definitely needed some new clothes, and when she made it back, she would look for a better apartment, a bigger apartment. She couldn't think about not having a job. She wanted to leave as soon as she could to see if she could find something, anything. She hadn't heard from the Times yet about the open position, and that worried her. From what Tawnya said a few weeks ago, one of the applicants that free-lanced before would fill the position.

She shook off her worries and started to worry about something else. Warren. She didn't want to leave things the way they were, she knew he must've overheard her and her father's conversation yesterday. She wanted to call him, to see how he was doing, but decided against it. Instead, she called the airline. Her plane would be in that Friday at five p.m. Four more days of Connecticut then back home. Funny how it didn't sound as good as it used to. She thought of him at least fifty times a day. The way he felt to her, the way his kisses pressed against her body. God, he was attentive. She stood, picked the paperwork up and headed out the door. She had a few errands to run. She didn't need a ride after all. Walking would do her good. She didn't need any more lectures on her love life.

The warm breeze outside did little for her as she was walking. Sweat travelled down her back into her beltline. She felt oddly heavy as she walked to the post office down town. The downside of walking was the post office being so close to Warren's house. Maybe she would stop to see how he was doing. Subconsciously her body carried her there. She didn't need to send the papers right away, but she supposed there was a reason for everything and tonight she had to see him.

She completely forgot about stopping at the drug store, which in this case should have been the first thing she did. Her birth control pills were running low and she didn't want to wait to get them until she went back to New York. *Not that I'll need them there*, she thought. As she came around the corner of Fifth and Rosedale, she saw his home.

His car wasn't in the drive, but she saw a light on through the window. He must've parked his car in the garage. She pressed the doorbell and heard the faint sound of it through the outside. "Coming," he yelled.

He opened the door and his eyes rounded. "Katherine?"

"Yeah, I thought I would stop by and..."

"Warren, could you get in here, I need help with this

damn zipper!" A woman's voice called from the bathroom.

Katherine's eyes widened, "I, Oh…" she took a deep breath. "I can see that I'm interrupting something." She turned to leave as she saw Warren's face redden as if he finally figured what that *something* was.

"Katherine, don't go," Warren called after her, grabbing her arm.

"I can see you work fast! You son of a bitch! Here I was feeling awful, guilty even. I came over here to apologize!"

"Warren, can you…," the other woman said as she came around the corner. Her smile went into a line and looked at Warren.

"Sydney, could you just hold on for a damn minute! Come here, I want you to meet someone."

"What the hell do you think you're doing? I don't want to meet your…"

"Meet who exactly?" a beautiful blonde with legs to her ears walked around the corner dressed in a tight black number with the zipper all the way down to her waist. Missing a bra no less.

"Nice, Warren! How old is she?" Katherine spat.

"Warren chuckled back a laugh as he looked at the tall blonde. "The secret's out, Syd."

"What secret, who is this?" Sydney said smiling.

"Who am I? Who are you? Are you another wife, or…" she got quiet at the look at Warren's face. She shouldn't have gone there. Her eyes averted then turned.

"I'm," Sydney started, a little startled at the sudden outburst.

"This is my *sister*, Sydney. Sydney, this is Katherine. Katherine Daniels, we are in one of those 'no relationship' relationships... you know the kind that I'm talking about?" He smiled a small smile, hoping Katherine would turn around.

Katherine blanched at his words then turned, red faced embarrassed. "I'm so sorry. I... nice to meet you, Sydney."

Sydney smiled then realized her dress wasn't latched yet. "Warren, please?" Then she turned and he zipped her dress. "Hot date tonight... I'm twenty-five, by the way," she giggled at Warren. He shook his head. Katherine winced. "Looks like I'm interrupting the start of something hot myself. Nice to meet you, Katherine. Warren," she giggled then grabbed her purse and car keys and turned for the door.

Warren looked over the threshold at the woman standing before him. "You coming in, or do you want to make a scene? I'm up for it if you are." His eyes twinkled as he stood there. "By the way, you need to pay the toll; I heard a faint apology back there."

She smiled faintly then walked through the door, "Warren, I'm so embarrassed. I didn't mean what I said. I don't know what's gotten into me."

"You meant it. Women like you don't say things unless you mean it. You were just wrong this time. I deserved it. That's what you get when you aren't honest from the beginning. Although I didn't mean to hurt you, I must have."

"Well, obviously I hurt you yesterday morning. You left so quickly."

"Yeah, well, I heard what you said."

She winced. She thought he must have.

"I don't see why you're denying the obvious. We have

chemistry, we work well together, you and I. You only get so many chances at love, Katherine. Trust me, I know." *Love.* She felt it in his look, his touch, the tension in the room.

"Warren, you can't…"

"Whether you want me to or not, Katherine, it happened. And yes, I do love you. I love you."

She looked away from his eyes, not wanting to see the love in them for her. She didn't deserve it.

"I…"

"Have to go? I thought as much," he bent down to kiss her on the head. "I'll miss you. Please be careful in New York." His voice gave out on the last word making it almost inaudible.

"Warren," she pleaded, not knowing what was coming next. Tears streamlined down her face. She had been doing that a lot lately. He walked out of the room then into his bedroom. *God, I've made a mess of things.* She pulled at her hair in frustration. She didn't want to leave. She couldn't understand it. He gave her the out she needed, but she couldn't take it, not this way. She felt comfortable here, at home.

She couldn't concentrate upstairs, looking at all of his wife's flowers and pretty things, so she opened the door to the basement and walked down. She looked around at his things. So many of his possessions reminded her of herself. She liked the same things he did, listened to the same type of music. They really did connect. She wondered if she did love him. She guessed she always knew, from the moment when she first saw him, and when they first touched. The feeling that she had then was just as strong as it was now, and he didn't deny it, so why would she? Because she only had four days left, that's why. But she didn't have a job any more, and the Herald *was* hiring. *Oh, God, not her, too. The Herald?* What a joke. She went over to his movie collection and found one of her favorites, "Serendipity". The movie choice was anything but ironic. She started the DVD as she heard his bedroom door open.

Warren ran his hands through his hair and shook his head. The woman was just like her father, stubborn. He knew that going into it. He stood up and opened the bedroom door, then heard the surround sound from his basement. "What the hell?" He opened the door, and ran down the steps, "Date not go so well, Syd?"

"No, it didn't," Katherine said meekly.

"Katherine," Warren said. He thought his heart would leap. She was still there. "What are you doing? I thought…"

"I know… I just couldn't go like that. I'm sorry."

Warren choked back and pointed to his lips. She came across the room in a rush as he held his arms out. She hugged him as tight as he hugged her. They stood there, feelings pouring out of them. "I'm so glad you stayed. I didn't think I would see you again."

He bent down to kiss her. The kiss was rushed, hard; he wanted to show her how much he wanted her, how glad he was that she stayed. "I don't want to think about that," she said, coming up for air. "I just want to be here with you. I only have four days and I want them to be making love with you."

Warren sighed, and pulled her in closer, "No more talking about leaving," he said, kissing her once again. She could feel it all the way down to her toes. This man knew how to kiss. "I love you so much."

She swallowed hard. There it was again. When she heard him say it she knew it was true. She could feel it from his heart, see it in his eyes. She deepened their kiss and wrapped her arms around his neck. He stumbled backwards to the couch and lay down on his back with her arms still around him. Their hands were wild tugging at each other's clothes. He pulled at her shirt and she went straight for his belt. "Make love to me," she whispered. "I...I love you, Warren."

He took her face in his hands, his eyes were warm and he kissed her lips. "I love you," he said. Then his arms went down to her sides, feeling down her skin. She looked down her eyelashes, smiling at him. Her eyes were seductive, bedroom eyes.

He finished with the last button on her shirt and brought it down her back. She wore a pink lace bra that shaped her breasts nicely. "You're trying to kill me, aren't you?" His hands went to the back where the clasps were and pulled it off her. She was so damn beautiful. She moaned as he took her in his mouth.

As she straddled him, he moved her pants down her legs slowly, and she kicked them the rest of the way off. Then his hands went to her matching panties, and slowly revealed her center. His fingers slowly made their way to her core, making her squirm. Her breathing was ragged, her breast heaved as he felt his way inside of her. His tongue ravaged her body, sending chills down her spine. She was only too aware of her body around him. He sent her sensations down her skin that she'd never felt before.

***

"Mmm," Warren said, smiling as he brought his lips to hers. "We will definitely have to do that again." Pulling her into his arms tightly, she lay on top of him still.

"Mm-hmm." She sighed. "This is my new favorite place in your house."

"Definitely, and you are so perfect right here." He nuzzled his nose against her forehead, making her laugh. "You can't go back, Katherine. This feel's so right."

She looked up to see his smiling face and felt bad for what she was about to say. "You know this can't be anything more than what it is right now, don't you? As much as I like being with you, I have my own life in New York."

"Like? A little while ago you said you loved me," he said smoothing her hair away from her face. Her nose scrunched up. "Only one thing is keeping you away from me right now… very easy to remedy. You can work here. Writers can work anywhere, and a place? I have just the solution for you," he said as he gestured with his hand to his surroundings. "See, I've got it all figured out, now I just need you on board." He smiled at her as she looked up at the ceiling, forming the right words to say. *Bap Kennedy* sang in the background to the song *Moonlight kiss.*

"You know, Warren, doctors I hear are pretty much able to work anywhere, too. And why is it that I have to change my whole world upside down, and you don't have to do anything? Do you think it will be that easy? Finding a job is harder than you think."

"The Herald is hiring," he said nonchalantly.

"I am so sick of hearing about the damn Herald!"

142

Warren jumped. "You can't be serious. I'm a serious journalist, the Herald is nothing compared to what I wa... am making right now. No thanks."

He noticed her hesitate, but thought nothing of it. "I make plenty of money for both of us. There's so much more to life than money. What about happiness?"

"Sure, but it looks like only one of us will be happy. I'm sorry, Warren. Obviously, this isn't a good idea. We work well in bed, but..."

"Don't say that. You know that isn't true," he said as his pager went off. He picked his pants off the floor and reached in his pocket. He looked down at the number then sat up quickly, practically knocking Kat to the floor. He grabbed the phone and dialed.

"This is Warren, is everything okay?"

"Complications, his heart started racing and he can't seem to get his air. We're on our way to the hospital right now. We can't find, Kat. Is she there with you?"

"Yes, she is... she's standing right next to me. Do you want to talk to her?"

"No, just bring her to the hospital with you. We'll see you soon." The phone clicked and he turned to look at her. She already knew by the look in his eyes that something was wrong.

"It's your dad again, Katherine. Heart problems, we have to go now." She nodded quickly, throwing on her clothes.

He was like a father to him, a best friend. He certainly didn't know what he would do without him. He had to fix it. They pulled into the hospital emergency room ten minutes later. Kat wasted no time getting out of the car, running through the emergency room doors. Her mother and father were nowhere to be seen. Warren, close behind, ran in and pushed a button on the side wall of the small waiting area. He grabbed a clipboard off a nearby wall, then looked towards the nurse's desk. A few of the nurse's heads peaked up from their computers looking towards him and one even pointed towards a room. Warren nodded his head and said thanks. Then turned to Kat. "Come on, you can come in, too."

When they walked into the room, Bill and Gail's heads turned. Bill smiled as he saw his daughter peek in. Warren walked over to the attending Doctor and pulled him to the side. "What's his chart look like, Patterson?"

"Warren, that's the thing. He came in pulling at his chest. It's only indigestion. Has he been following the diet that you had outlined for him? I was just getting ready to talk with him."

"That's not necessary, Patterson. If you don't mind, I will take over from here. I've been fighting with Bill for weeks on this. I would like to talk to him, if you don't mind."

"No, not at all. I hear we have a full house tonight, anyway. You going to be here all night, too?"

"No, I was paged. I had a night planned." Warren saw Patterson look to his side, noticing the brunette standing near him and smiled.

"Looks like you had a great night planned. Good luck," he said with a wink then handed the clipboard over to Warren.

"What was that all about, Warren?" Kat said. She put her hand on his shoulder, turning him towards her. "Is my father going to be alright?" She looked worried. Her forehead started to wrinkle; she looked from him to her father.

"Actually, I need you all to leave the room. I need to talk with your father, alone."

"No, I don't think so. Whatever it is you can tell all of us," she said, looking flustered.

"No, actually I can't, Hi..."

"Hippa laws forbid it, blah blah blah, it's my father."

Bill Daniels smiled. "It's okay, doc, you know my Kat. Very protective. So, am I going to live?"

Warren almost started to laugh as he looked at Bill. He then took his clipboard and swatted his friend in the shoulder. The two women in the room exchanged nervous glances. "Damn it, Bill! How many times do I have to tell you to follow your diet? No more eggs, no more bacon, and if I see any grease at all on your fingertips I am going to kill you myself!" Warren yelled. Gail Daniels looked up; her eyes were wide then turned them on her husband.

"What did you do, Bill?"

"I... Doc, what are you trying to do here?" Bill asked.

"I'm trying to do my job, Bill. You have to follow your diet. You will not live if you don't. You didn't have a heart attack, or even a close call. You had indigestion! If you don't start obeying the diet, you won't live to see your grandchildren grow!" Bill and Gail turned their heads in Katherine's direction.

"What? Oh, God, don't look at me! I'm not even married!" She looked shocked at the rudeness. Bill and Gail turned to Warren.

"Warren, I'm sorry," Gail said. "I would like to have a

copy of this diet now. I will make sure Bill follows it to the letter, won't I, Bill?"

"Yes, ma'am," Bill said, turning a mean glare on Warren.

"Well, I will get your discharge papers, and you can get dressed. Remember, Bill, follow the diet. Gail, I suggest no salt, and let him get used to the idea of bland foods for now." Warren walked out of the room and to the nurse's station. Katherine and her mother then started in on Bill.

"William Michael Daniels!" Gail said in her best disapproving mother voice...

Bill threw up his arms and glanced to the ceiling and said, "Pack your bags, were going on a guilt trip."

"This isn't funny, Dad," Kat joined in. "I was worried sick and I'm sure everyone else was, too."

"Do I have big buck teeth sticking out of my mouth?" Bill started. Katherine and Gail looked at each other, obviously not seeing what he was getting at. "How am I supposed to eat all that rabbit scratch?"

Katherine rolled her eyes, "It seems like an easy choice, dad. Plain oatmeal or death."

"I'll take death by chocolate!" Bill said excitedly with a big grin. Kat opened her mouth in shock that her father would be so glib about this whole thing, then she heard a snicker; her mother was stifling a laugh. Soon the whole room erupted in laughter. Gail leaned forward and gave Bill a kiss on the cheek.

She spoke into his ear, "You're impossible, you old coot. Come on, let's get you home." Warren walked back in and Gail straightened up.

"Alright everyone, time to go home; here are your

papers." He handed the papers to Bill, and he signed them. Gail smiled at Warren as she left the room; Katherine waited with him as he filed his paper work.

"Thank you, Warren."

He turned towards her, and put his hand up to her cheek, noticing the women sitting at the desk behind him and put his hand back down. "You're welcome." Katherine smiled back at him as she took his hand in hers. "Is four days going to be enough?" She sighed.

"No, but I'll take it." He knew that four days would be all he would need to convince her to stay. She had a lot more here than she thought she did. Family, friends, a history. Not to mention the way she made him feel just knowing that she was in the same room with him. He walked with her back down the hallway, pushing the emergency room doors open in silence. He held the outer door open for her as she walked to his truck. As they settled themselves in, he turned the key over, grabbed a CD out of the console and slid it into the player. The music was a mix of songs that he'd made that reminded him of her. A few oldies intermixed with pop. The first song was Santana's *Black Magic Woman*. Katherine must have liked the song, too; she tapped the beat out rhythmically on her knee as she looked out the window. He drove a little bit further in silence, then pulled over.

Katherine turned her head in his direction. "Is something wrong?"

"You haven't said two words to me since we left the hospital, you tell me."

She looked around the vehicle, taking notice of the way Warren's body tensed, as she didn't give him her full attention. "You haven't said anything to me, either. I just thought you were enjoying your music, that's all."

His shoulders eased. "Oh, sorry, this CD helps me relax."

"Yeah, I can see that," she joked. He smiled, "Santana is one of my favorites." She laughed nervously and went to cover it up with her hand. Then more laughter erupted as tears streamed down her face.

Warren laughed, too, not having a clue as to why she was laughing, then seeing the sight of tears in her eyes, he pulled her into him.

"Are you okay, what's wrong?"

"God, nothing, and everything, I suppose. I just find all of this humorous; you here with me. We don't know each other; I'm worrying about a measly four days, like an idiot."

That was the furthest thing from his mind. He'd been thinking about her for months. He knew her. She didn't want to admit it, but she knew him, too. "I don't think you're an idiot at all. I think we're going to have a great time these next few days. Don't worry; you'll know what you want when you walk away from here."

"I know what I want, Warren."

"Do you?" he asked as he brushed a stray hair from her face. She moved away from the contact and looked back out the window.

"I want to be a writer for the *New York Times*. I want to do more freelance work. I want to move into a bigger apartment, so I can stop the ridicule from Bill and Gail."

Warren scoffed as she rattled off the last bit. Just his luck. For the first time in a long time he'd fallen in love, and the woman in his life could only think of herself. That's what they said about history repeating itself. He turned the key over once again and drove to Bill and Gail's. He couldn't think of anything to do with her now. She turned to face him as they drove around the corner. "I thought... I thought we were going back to your place. Four more days, remember?" she said nervously.

His shoulders stiffened again as he pulled up the drive and put his truck in park. He took a deep breath, and looked straight ahead of him. "If you want to go out with me, I'll pick you up at seven."

"Oh, I just... I thought... seven. Thanks for the lift, I'll be... what should I wear?"

"Whatever you want. I'll be here at seven," he said, not looking at her.

"Warren? Whatever it is you're mad at, I'm sorry," she said as she stepped out and opened the door to her parents' home.

Warren placed his head in his hands and let out a deep breath. This was going to be a lot harder than he thought. It was going to take a lot of convincing if he was going to make her stay.

CHAPTER NINE

As Katherine walked into her parent's house, her father greeted her almost immediately at the door. "What are you doing here?" he asked inquisitively.

"What? Do you want me to leave?" she asked.

"No, sorry, hon, I just thought... where's Warren?" he asked. Gail walked out of the kitchen towards the two, wiping her hands on an old dish towel. She smiled as she put her arms around her husband's waist and kissed his neck.

"Everything okay, Katherine? Her mother asked. She smiled as she watched how happy her parents were.

"Yes, everything is fine. Warren is getting ready; we're going out this evening. He's picking me up at seven."

"See Gail, I told you he was a smart boy. Asking our Kat out on a date," Bill boasted. "You'll see. He's a good man, Kat."

"I never said he wasn't. It's only three dates, then I leave. Don't go securing a church."

"Did you hear that, Gail? Three dates now...not just one! Warren's a good man. I'm going to have to let him use that new pole I just bought. I never thought he had the gumption to ask for three dates." Gail laughed as Kat rolled her eyes.

"As I said, it's just three dates. Then I'm going back to New York, so don't go getting your hopes up; just a good time between two friends. Now if you don't mind, I'm going to go to my room to find something to wear.

***

Warren Vance hadn't been out on a date in over five years. The last time he went on a date, corduroys and vests were still in style. It's not that he didn't know what to wear; he was actually a pretty snappy dresser. But he didn't know how to impress women. He surely wasn't that impressive thus far, or she would have agreed to a little more than three dates. And with only four days until she leaves, he was just about out of time. He thought about the one source he used while in college; the women's romance collection. His wife, Sarah had loved watching her romantic films. "When Harry met Sally," "You've got mail," "Sleepless in Seattle." Basically any romance with Meg Ryan. *Meg Ryan, now there was a gal,* he thought.

Katherine was a little like her. She was the girl next door type. She wasn't into fancy dressing or high dollar items. That he had seen... at least from the impression that Bill gave him of her in their endless chats. She wasn't used to being romanced. Every woman that he had ever met, or talked to, had talked about *Romance*; the man that never gave it, or losing the romance after marriage. He used to talk to his secretary about her and her husband's love life. The romance at the beginning was always very spontaneous. He would buy her roses, perfume, even once the man actually had the nerve to play a song on the guitar for her outside of her apartment building. She said it was the most god-awful thing she had ever heard; some of the people opened their windows and cursed at him. He even had a jar of peanut butter and a cup of what appeared to be either tomato juice or blood thrown at him, yet he played on. That was what done her in. Her eyes would always flutter at that point. Warren would always laugh. That's what he had to do, impress her somehow. *Impressions, that's it!* There was a store down on the corner of Mill and Howard. Real fancy, women like clothes…. shoes…glitter… and dancing… He picked up the phone and got started. She was surely not to forget the night that he had planned for them.

***

The doorbell rang shortly after 6:00 p.m. Gail Daniels promptly answered the door, smiling at the man on the other side. "Yes," she said.

"Hi, Ma'am. I am just making a delivery. Are you Katherine Daniels?"

"No, I'm her mother; she's in the other room. Shall I get her?"

"That's okay. I am just to make sure that she gets this dress," he said as he handed her the long-hanging bag. Gail smiled at the man as he went to leave; she called out for him to wait so she could tip him. Noticing the word, "Impressions" on the bag, she smiled and walked back to bang on Katherine's door.

"Katherine! Special delivery!" she yelled. The door opened and Katherine stood their looking at the bag…

"What's this?" she asked, noting the smile on her mom's face.

"I don't know. It was just delivered to our door for you. I think it's from Warren!"

"Impressions?" she asked. "This must have cost a fortune!"

"I know! When I saw the bag I about lost it. Your father won't even let me park my car near the sidewalk. He says the smell of *expensive* is in the air and just breathing it in will empty his bank account!"

Katherine laughed, then quickly grabbed the bag and took it over to the bed and unzipped it. Inside was the most beautiful emerald green gown that she had ever seen. Gorgeous. Cut into a low V and a cinched waist, the gown flowed all the way down to her feet. Then she heard the doorbell again. Katherine and her mom exchanged glances, Gail ran to the door. "You don't think?" she said giddily.

"Hi, Ma'am, I'm from Duttons. I was asked to personally deliver this to a Ms. Katherine Daniels."

"Thank you very much, young man," Gail said, as she grabbed her purse once again, leaving a small tip for the boy. He nodded his head in appreciation and walked out the door. She ran back down the hallway to Katherine, launching the newest arrival into her hands.

"Warren?" she asked

"Do you know anyone else?"

"No!" Kat laughed. She opened the box and inside was the cutest pair of size 8 strappy heels. Perfect. She pulled off her socks and put one foot in the shoe. "It's a perfect fit!"

"Just like Cinderella!" her mom squealed. Katherine laughed. "Try on the dress! Let me feel it first! Oh, my God it's Ralph Lauren!"

"Shit! How much do you think this cost?" Katherine asked her mother, stripping down and trying to pull the dress over her head.

"I don't know, but I am going to find out. Give me that phone!"

"MOM!"

"Fine. I am going over to that store though; your father is not going to get away with this!"

"Away with what?"

"I've been married for forty-two years, Katherine! I have never had anything remotely this…"

Doorbell.

"What do you suppose that is?" Katherine beamed. The two exchanged glances. They both squeezed through the bedroom door and raced to the foyer. They stopped; Katherine took a breath and turned the knob. "Yes?"

"Hello, Ma'am. Wow… You look," he stammered, mouth agape, looking down her body.

Man, maybe she should dress like this more often. Although, the boy had to have been no older than seventeen, and he called her ma'am. *Mrs. Robinson? Nah…*

"Thank you, is there something you need?"

"Well, yes, sorry…" He blushed. "I have a delivery from Wilsons. A Dr. Warren Vance wanted me to deliver it to you with this message," he said as he handed her two boxes; one long and one short, then handed her an envelope before he turned around.

"Thanks," she said.

"Wait!" Gail Daniels yelled. She grabbed her purse, and handed the boy some money and he ran out the door to his car. "You owe me twenty bucks, Katherine."

Katherine laughed.

"What's inside? Oh, my God, Wilsons!"

Katherine opened the envelope first, and it read:

All that glitters is gold, is a timeless expression. I wanted you to have something even better. Emeralds for the color of your beautiful eyes, eyes that I want to look into all night while we're having dinner, and dancing. See you at seven.

Yours,
Warren

"My God," she said, then promptly picked up the short box first. Opening it, she saw a pair of gorgeous emerald earrings, an emerald in the center surrounded by nine diamonds. She gasped as she looked at them; her mother let out a shriek. She had an odd sense of déjà vu looking at the earrings. There was something about the emerald with the nine diamonds around it. *Hmm*, she thought. She put her hand to her heart and looked down once again. She and her mom glanced towards the other box; Kat quickly grabbed it and opened it up. It was the same pattern as the earrings, only it was a long chain and one singular emerald inlay surrounded by diamonds. It was stunning. "Damn!"

"Oh, my God! I am going to kill your father!" Gail muttered. "What's the note say?"

"Here," Katherine said breathlessly, handing her mother the note. She read it aloud; a little tear came down her cheek.

"That is so... so... romantic!" she cried. Katherine didn't say anything. She just went through the motions, putting the earrings and necklace on.

"I shouldn't accept this. It's beautiful, but it's just too

much." She knew as soon as she said it that she would never give it up. It was beautiful, and it was perfectly Warren.

Gail Daniel's hand wrapped her on the forehead. "Are you insane? Warren is quite the catch! He gives you a dress, earrings, necklace, and shoes for Christ Sake, and you're going to throw it back in his face?"

"Mom!" Katherine yelled. In her entire life, she had never heard her mother, the devout Christian, take the Lord's name in vain. She was shocked.

"Well, I'm just saying, Katherine, that it's rude." Then she stood up and walked towards the door. "If you need help with your hair, I have some bobby pins and a very nice rhinestone barrette that will do the trick. It's in my bathroom drawer." Gail smiled once again, shook her head and muttered curses under her breath.

Katherine could hear a few words like *damn* and *Bill.* She was sure that this would not be good for him.

An hour later, Kat stepped out of the bathroom into the hallway. Her father saw her and gasped, put his hand up to his chest, and rocked back on his heels. Kat ran over to him to see if he was alright. "Dad, Dad, are you alright? Mom, call the hospital!" she screamed.

"Gail, don't you do such a thing! Katherine Elizabeth Daniels, you steal my breath. You look stunning in that green color, only it does come down way too far in the front," he grumbled to the side. "Gail, get your daughter a smock!" he yelled. They all laughed.

"Daddy, I'm wearing this, and don't you do that with your hand again, you scared the hell out of me!"

"Language, Katherine," her mother said. *This coming*

from the woman that just took the Lord's name in vain, not to mention the mutterings about her father and how she was going to kill him.

"Sorry, mom, I'll try to control myself."

Gail looked at her daughter appraisingly, and then saw Warren through the sidelight by the door. "He's here," she whispered. "And, he looks great."

"Katherine turned around and walked towards the door while her father opened it. Warren stood there; his eyes moved down her body appraisingly. Her father swatted him at the chest.

"Damn, Bill!"

Katherine's mom tsked. "Sorry, Gail,"

"Well, son, she's still my daughter! I don't care if she's old as dirt!"

"Daddy!" Katherine scolded.

Warren laughed. "Shall we get going?" he asked, as he pulled up his elbow; she grabbed it, and flung her head back.

"We shall. Bye, mom; bye, dad," she said as they walked out the door. Bill and Gail exchanged glances.

"Our baby, Gail, I think this may be it!"

"I think so, too. I can't believe he called for her dress size. He has great taste. Speaking of that, old man; I have a bone to pick with you."

"Oh geesh," Bill said as he rolled his eyes.

CHAPTER TEN

"**Y**ou are breathtaking, Katherine," Warren said as he took her hand and put it up to his lips. "Simply breathtaking."

"Thank you. You clean up pretty well yourself." Katherine smiled and took a deep breath. "Warren?"

"Yes," he said, looking to her.

"Thank you so much for the beautiful dress, the shoes and the gorgeous jewelry. I don't even want to think about how much it co—"

"Don't you worry about a thing," Warren interrupted. "I wanted you to have a perfect evening. How were you supposed to do that without the dress? Then you had to have shoes, and when I went past Wilsons, I couldn't resist." Warren put his hand on her neck and touched the necklace. "There they were the most beautiful necklace and earrings. They really do match your eyes."

Kat closed her eyes and leaned in to his palm.

"They don't do you justice, Kat. You're stunning."

"Thank you," Katherine said as she leaned in to kiss him. Warren put his fingers to her lips before they could seal their kiss.

"Not yet. I want to save this for us, not for them," Warren said, gesturing to Gail and Bill gaping out the window.

"You would think they've seen two people in," she caught herself. Warren exhaled and looked at her. "The driveway before, I mean really," she said, then looked down embarrassed.

Warren was going to say something, but decided against it. He knew exactly what she was going to say. "They're just checking up on us. It's not a big deal, but what I want to do with you, I would like to keep between us. Besides, I don't want your dad riding me about it next week on our fishing trip."

"Good point." Kat laughed as she turned back toward the window and stuck her tongue out. Her mom and dad scrambled from the window as if she couldn't see them. *As if!*

"Well, let's get going. Madame," Warren said, making a grand gesture for his SUV, "your chariot awaits."

"Thank you, sir," she replied in turn as she took his hand and stepped into his truck.

***

They arrived at the *Sirian Riverboat Cruise* port entrance and Katherine grinned. "Warren, are we going on the River?" Katherine said happily.

"We are, is there a problem?"

"Oh, God no. I always wanted to go on one. I just never had…"

"Anyone to go with?"

"Exactly. Did I thank you yet?"

"You did, but you can thank me again. A kiss maybe?"

"I thought you didn't want a thank you kiss."

"No, that's not it at all. I just wanted to have you all to myself. You know how your father can be." Warren smiled as he put his hand up to her face.

"Is that so? Well, how about I thank you for the riverboat cruise right now?" She pulled him into a kiss. Her lips brushed his as she brought her arms up around his neck. "And, maybe I should thank you for the earrings," she whispered into his ear, then nuzzled his neck. She kissed him gently as his hands went to her waist.

"God, you drive me crazy, Katherine," he said as his hands went up her back. "You have got to stop that or we won't be going on that cruise."

Katherine laughed then pulled back, "Okay, you asked for it, no more thank-you."

Warren's smile disappeared, and a playful look took its place. "Oh, no you don't," he said as he pulled her back. "I still need one more kiss, and later you can really thank me when we get back to my place."

"Your place? Well, Dr. Vance, I thought this was our first date. You can't possibly think that I would sleep with someone on the first date?"

"Well technically, my dear Katherine, we won't be sleeping." Warren smiled and kissed her neck once more. A little moan escaped her mouth, then she straightened her back, and smiled. "Now can we get on that boat? I'm starving." She took his arm and he led her to the dock.

***

After eating dinner and dancing, Katherine and Warren retired to the seating area of the riverboat. They talked about politics, her father's heart, and her living situation in New York. Warren, of course, reminded her every two seconds that he lived in a big house all by himself and Katherine let him know how happy she was in New York. *As if.* She was never really all that happy. Although she didn't like the size of her apartment, it was never about that. She liked her independence. She made a life for herself away from her parents. Not one of her siblings had done so; they all lived within a hands reach from them. It wasn't that she didn't like her parents, she adored them. She just wanted to be able to say that she made it on her own, and if even for a second she thought that she could spend more time with Warren without having Gail and Bill breathing down her neck, she would.

A hand tapped her on the shoulder and two faces came into view: Jean and Paul, from the plane ride. Kat smiled at them and stood up. Jean wrapped her arms around her.

"You look beautiful; I almost didn't recognize you! Not that you weren't beautiful on the plane," Jean said, recovering. Paul nodded and smiled, too. Then they noticed Warren, and Jean grinned. "Who's your friend?"

Kat laughed and Warren stood. "Hi, I'm Warren." He held his hand out. Jean laughed and hugged him, too.

"Anyone that can put a smile on Kat's face after her horrendous month deserves a hug! It's nice to meet you, Warren. This is my fiancé, Paul." Jean smiled and Paul put his hand out.

"I don't do hugs." Paul laughed. So did Warren and Kat.

"That's good... I don't touch men."

"Well, good for you," Jean said, winking and nudging Kat in the side. "So, how long have you both known each other? We saw you on the dance floor earlier, and you look great together."

Warren smiled at that, and turned to look at Katherine. "Now, see she knows you for how long and *she* knows?" Warren smiled.

"Don't start," Kat joked, and then looked at Jean. "He's my father's doctor. He's the one that picked me up at the airport."

Not exactly the introduction he hoped for, however, he would take anything, but friend at this point, something that she kept insinuating that they were.

"Oh," Jean said, amused. "A *doctor*."

Paul rolled his eyes. "Her mother is always telling her she should have married one. I swear if she could put me through medical school on her waitressing salary she would have."

"Now, Paul, she likes you. She just likes doctors better." Jean laughed at the look Paul gave Warren.

"Help me out, buddy."

"You tell your mother-n-law-to-be that being a doctor isn't all that glamorous. You're on call all of the time. How are you supposed to take care of her the way you want if you're always at work?"

Paul laughed and replied, "That's probably why she wants me to switch professions!"

They sat together for the rest of the evening. Warren didn't seem annoyed or put out by the interruption. Paul and Jean were great, too; they talked about their vacation and genuinely seemed interested in meeting up when Kat returned to New York. They invited Warren, too. He seemed to win them over as much as he won her over. His smiles could undo anyone. He was infectious.

As the night wore down, they said their goodbyes to Jean and Paul, and Warren took her hand and walked along the shoreline with her. The moon was full, and the stars were in full view. It was nothing like New York, no high rises, no big steel structures, just the beauty of the river and the walkway where they strolled hand-in-hand. They didn't need music, or conversation. This was the most comfortable she had felt with any man, and that's why it was going to be so hard to leave. All she could think of was what a big mistake it was getting involved with him when they only had a short time.

The night with Warren was magical. He wined, dined, and romanced the hell out of her. She had never experienced anything remotely like this. As they walked to his truck, he opened the door for her to get in and kissed the tip of her nose, then he walked over to his side. "I had a wonderful time with you tonight, Katherine," he said as he started the engine. "I hope you enjoyed it as well."

"Are you kidding me? Warren, this was the most perfect night," she said as she smiled and glanced out the window. "Everything was perfect, the dress, the shoes, which, I must say don't even hurt my feet at all, and the jewelry... dear God, I love it!" she said as she held her hand to her chest where the necklace laid. "Is it wrong to say that?" She laughed nervously.

"No. I was hoping that you didn't have anything like it. When I saw the necklace, I knew you had to have it. It looks just like your eyes."

"The funny thing is, Warren, I feel like it's been mine for a lifetime already. It's beautiful. It looks so familiar to me, almost as if it was mine before. I know that sounds crazy, but I am so grateful for them. Thank you so much. I have never received something so beautiful in my life."

"You're most welcome." He turned down her street when she let out a sigh. "Is everything okay?"

"Well, yes, I just don't know what to say. I suppose should feel guilty for accepting the jewelry."

"Don't. Like you said, it was made for you. Besides, you don't really want to give it back, do you?"

It was her turn to laugh now. "Hell no!"

"I'm glad. I think it would have killed me to have to take that back into Wilsons. Well, my dear, sit tight," he said as he turned off his truck and walked over to her door.

"I didn't even realize we were at my house. I thought you were going to demand thanks for the night from me?" she asked coyly.

"You don't owe me anything. I'm just glad that you said yes to tonight. I can't wait to see you tomorrow. I wanted this night to be perfect, and to me, it was just as any first date should be. Now, take my hand, I'm going to walk you to your door."

Katherine inhaled deeply, feeling nervous for the first time that evening, which considering was probably rather foolish since she had already slept with this man, or technically as Warren put it, had sex. Now she had butterflies, wondering if he would kiss her goodnight, before shoving her through the door to hell a.k.a. Bill and Gail Daniels.

"Thank you again for the lovely evening," Warren said.
"Thank—"

Warren leaned in. Her breath stopped, and he brushed his lips against hers, tasting her, devouring her kiss. She wanted him. She couldn't believe how bad she wanted him. The night had been so perfect already.

"Take me back to your place," she said huskily.

Warren moaned into her mouth. "I wanted this night to be perfect for you. I didn't want to ruin it…"

"Ruin it?" She shook herself out of the daze which was the perfect evening. "How would that ruin it?"

"I just—it wouldn't—I just didn't want to pressure you. You were so sure that this would only be three dates…"

"Right, sorry. I don't want to hurt you, Warren."

"That's not it at all. I just didn't think…"

"No, you're right. I don't know what I was thinking, taking it further with only three dates in mind would have been…immature. We're adults, and I think we can handle each other's friendship. We're just friends."

"Katherine, I think you know that we're more than just friends."

"No, well, yes, I know that we slept together."

"Made love," Warren interjected.

"Had sex," Kat said, immediately regretting it as she registered Warren's face.

"And here I thought I was going to ruin the evening?" Warren's face was ashen in embarrassment. He leaned in once more and kissed her cheek. "Good night. Tomorrow night, 8'oclock?"

"Warren…"

A movement caught her attention behind Warren, and something dropped down the wall and landed in the bushes. She sucked in a startled gasp, but calmed down when she saw what it was.

"Tommy?"

"Kat?" Tommy Jones' voice called from the other side of the yard, his face flush. Warren looked over and nodded to him.

"Warren," Tommy said, nodding back. "Kat, don't you say anything to her, you hear me!"

"To whom?"

Warren rolled his eyes and shook his head. "Eight o'clock," he said before he got into his SUV and drove off.

"Wait, Warren!" she huffed, and then turned and glared at Tommy like it was his fault Warren left. Tommy acted oblivious to the glare and pulled his cell phone from his pocket. "*To whom?*" she repeated.

Tommy looked up, "To whom, who?"

"Don't say anything to whom!" she said, loudly.

"Your sister!"

"*My sister?*" Kat said. She looked above the bushes to her sister's window, and then straightened. "No... Tommy Jones, what did you do?"

"I didn't do anything. Just don't say anything. She will be too embarrassed. She has enough going on with you and Warren making out every two seconds." He made some gestures by squishing his hands together a few times.

"We haven't been making out every two seconds, and what did you do to my sister?"

Tommy took a step back and his eyes widened. "*I didn't do anything* to your sister. Honestly, Kat, give me some credit. I would never do anything to hurt your sister. Never. God, what kind of... never mind, I'm getting out of here. Just don't say anything." He flipped open his cell phone dramatically before turning away.

"Whatever!" she yelled back as she watched him walk down the sidewalk towards the road. Who the hell was he talking to at this hour on a cell phone? Not to mention,

166

where was his car? And, what the hell was he doing sniffing around her sister's bedroom? As far as she knew, Karen had enough problems with her crazy boyfriends. The last thing she needed was to throw Tommy Jones into the mix.

When Kat turned the key in the lock, the kitchen light immediately turned on followed by her mother walking into the kitchen and her father directly behind her with a small dinner plate. "What are you doing here?" Bill asked.

"Well, last time I checked I was staying here. What's with everyone tonight?"

"What's with whom?" Gail asked.

Deciding that she probably shouldn't say anything about Tommy crawling out of her sister's bedroom window, Kat just shook her head.

"Nothing...I just...I just got here."

"Did you have a nice time, dear?" Gail said as she pulled out a chair to sit down and brought the small dinner plate with her and motioned for Bill with the other hand. He came around with the cookie jar grasped in his hands. Kat reached over, helped her father with the jar and placed it on the table before she realized what she did. "Wait, you shouldn't be eating cookies! Mom, what are you doing?"

"Well, he was very good tonight, weren't you, dear?" Gail asked Bill.

"Oh, God! Mom, dad, enough already. You're the ones that have to live with yourselves if his blood pressure acts up again..."

"Don't you worry about my blood pressure, what happened with your date tonight? Are you going to move back into the old homestead?"

Gail rolled her eyes and swatted Bill with the back of her hand. "Bill, I hardly think she would move back in here! Don't you think she would live with Warren?"

"Not you, too! I would think you would have known by now that I am leaving. And, after tonight, I am convinced more than ever that I should get out of here. That's why I'm calling and booking a flight right away." Bill and Gail exchanged glances while Katherine picked apart a chocolate chip cookie.

"What do you mean you're booking a flight? What, are you leaving now?" Gail asked.

"Well, it's not like I have anything here. You guys have pushed me and Warren together. He's so delusional about our relationship. I told him and the both of you, that I like the way my life is. I like living in New York. I like writing." She looked down again and picked the chips absently out of the cookie. "I mean, don't you think he's being silly? You would think by the way he's been acting that we've known each other for years."

Gail closed her eyes and took a deep breath. "I don't think he's delusional at all, Katherine. Don't you think you are being a bit hard on him? When you find something you want, you go for it. He wants you. Isn't that what you want?"

Katherine laughed aloud as she looked up at her parents. "What *I* want? What *I* want? *I've* been telling you all this entire time! I want to write. I like my life. I like New York. I don't want to live in Connecticut my whole life and… and never get out!" she yelled. As she finished her tirade, her sister walked into the room and her face fell.

168

"I," Karen stammered, then shook her head and huffed. "I'm outta here. When you can get off your high horse, *princess*, give me a call!"

"My what?" Katherine stood up. Bill and Gail exchanged glances.

"You heard me! You think you're *so great* because you moved to New York? Because you got away? Well news flash, Katherine. This place that you think is the *depths of hell* is *great*. Mom and Dad live here, I live here, and so does Warren. A man that I might remind you that treats you so damn great, and what do you do? You throw it back in his face! You don't deserve him. You know what, you should go back to New York, and maybe some hard luck will hit you! Then when it does, give me a call and tell me how bad Warren and Connecticut sounds. Let me know how bad it sounds at two a.m. when you hear gun shots, or when you get humiliated the next time an article comes out. Can't wait to tell you I told you so!" Karen pulled her coat off the hook and stormed out the door.

Gail and Bill exchanged glances as Katherine shook her head. "Is this what you both think, too?" she asked. Her voice was a higher pitch at the end and her eyes tried like hell to bat the tears away.

"Well, Kitten," Bill began, "the way your sister said it,"

"Came out just right," Gail finished. She looked at her husband and squeezed his hand as they stood. "We love you, Katherine, but we aren't small minded people. We've been to other places..." Gail shook her head. "The way you talk sometimes, you'd think we acted like small town people, and maybe we do, but that doesn't mean that we're stupid, and neither is Karen. She just lacks tact."

Katherine huffed as she hugged her arms around her body. "I never said you were stupid," Katherine mumbled.

"You did, and we aren't. I'm sorry that you're embarrassed to be back here. Tell me exactly what we did that makes you fight so much to stay away?"

"There isn't... you didn't... I just... I want to do it for me. I want to do a lot of things, see the world... I'm still young. Why should I..."

"No you're not, Kat, and Warren knows what he wants. I think even Karen knows what she wants; she wants what all of us want, to *be* loved by someone that *you* love. She's really pissed that you have it and are throwing it away."

"She doesn't know anything!" Katherine said stubbornly.

"Do you?" Bill asked.

Katherine looked down and walked back to her bedroom and slammed the door.

***

The next morning she walked into the kitchen with her bags packed and her phone held firmly in her hand. Gail stood up and walked over to her. "Katherine, baby, don't go. Last night, Karen and I..."

"Mom, save it. It's okay. I didn't get a whole hell of a lot of sleep last night with the whole 'gang up on Kat thing' going. I don't appreciate it. I thought we could talk over the Warren problem. The date was, I don't know... I just. Well, the taxi is outside. Tell, Daddy I love him and give Karen a message for me. Tell her to make sure she locks her bedroom window to keep the riffraff out."

"Riffraff?" Karen squeaked from the hall.

"Oh, hi, Karen, did you get the message?" Kat asked as

she opened the door. "Good!" Kat turned with knob in her hand and slammed it.

As Kat walked out into the driveway, a few different things happened at once. First, she saw Tommy Jones crawling, once again, from her sister's bedroom window, and then she saw him smile and take a deep breath as he turned and placed his right hand to his heart, smiling.

"What the hell are you doing sniffing around my sister?"

He flinched. "Jesus H. Chri…"

"Tommy!" Kat said.

"Well, you scared me. What, are you taking up private investigating? I didn't do anything, see anything, or hear anything. Now drop it. By the way, I heard what you said to your sister, and I don't appreciate the comment about locking her window!"

"Ha, well, you should. She can be quite the—"

"You better watch yourself, Kat," Tommy interrupted.

"What? Do you *like* her or something?" Kat's eyes widened as she shook her head. "Oh, my God, Tommy Jones, you have a crush on my baby sister!" She started to laugh.

"What's so funny?"

Kat threw up her arms. "Oh, just about everything."

"Yeah, well, I don't think it's funny, and don't you worry about it."

"Does she know?"

"Does she know *what?*"

"That you are absolutely-head-over-heels-puppy-lovin' for her?" she said in the sweetest, gushiest voice she could muster.

"Damn it, Katherine, you are so immature."

"That's great coming from you, Tommy." Kat laughed "Where the hell is that taxi?"

"You need a ride?"

She rolled her eyes, thinking she had a decent chance that she wouldn't die if he took her, but if she waited much longer the whole family would be outside. "Could you?"

"Yeah, get in," Tommy said as he opened the door to his hatchback, "and put your seatbelt on."

Katherine laughed. "What's so funny about driving safely?" Tommy asked.

"Nothing, Tommy," she assured him. *Nothing at all.*

***

On the way over to the airport, Tommy took it slow— very slow. When she dated him in high school she thought he drove at a craw; just to put the moves on her, to make the night last longer. Here he was just extremely cautious. "I know what you should be when you grow up, Tommy?"

Tommy laughed. "What's that?"

"A Drivers ED instructor!" She laughed. "I have never seen anyone drive so slow in my entire life!"

"Yeah, well," Tommy said, checking his watch. He looked behind him in his mirror, and checked his watch twice more before he made the Airport turn.

"What are you doing? Are you expecting…? Tommy, tell me you didn't"

"What?"

"You didn't call Warren, did you?"

"Do you want me to tell you I didn't or tell you what I

did?" he winced.

She hit him on the shoulder with her purse. "Damn it! Why can't everyone just butt out! If I wanted to talk to him I would've called! This isn't anyone's business but my own!"

"Well, yours and Warren's."

"Tommy!"

"Well, sorry, I just. Don't worry; I called him before I saw you out in the drive. I don't think he's coming."

Katherine looked behind her shoulder and grimaced. She didn't think he was, either. And, in that weird way, it made her sad. She felt hurt, like he didn't care for her and she knew she didn't have the right to feel that way since she was, in fact, the one who was doing the leaving.

"Yeah," she said.

"Kat," Tommy said, "Are you okay?"

Kat started to cry. She pulled her hands up to her face and held herself up for a while. Tears streamed down as Tommy put his arm around her shoulders and found a parking space in the terminal.

"You wanna talk about it?"

"I don't. Think. I. Can!" she yelped, her crying made it difficult to talk.

"Well, I don't think what you're doing is necessarily a bad thing."

She turned her head quickly to face him. It was the first time someone, anyone at all agreed with her. She had to hear this. Her mascara was running down her face and her lipstick was all rubbed off onto her palms. She sniffed and tried to wipe her eyes without making the mascara worse. "Well?"

"Well, you haven't known each other for that long and, you are just being cautious. Look what happens when you don't know a person; take that Kelsey guy for instance."

Katherine began heaving now, and her yelps got louder. "Oh, God...I knew him for eight years!"

"Well now, you didn't really know him, did you? Wasn't that your first date?" Tommy asked quickly.

Katherine pulled her head up again, "Yes, but..."

"But, what? You didn't *really* know him. Maybe you need to put some distance between the both of you so you can figure out what you need, and then maybe he will figure out what he needs."

"You think so?" she squeaked out.

"Yeah, I mean, take me for example. I loved you all my life and I dated you and realized that when I slept with your sister she was much better than you. If I wouldn't have met her one night when she was drunk, I would still be hung up on the *wrong sister*, you see?"

"YOU WHAT?"

"Just kidding..." Tommy grinned.

"Tommy!" Kat laughed. "I could hit you sometimes!"

"Hey take it from me; I got some great advice from someone once. I don't know if this is a perfect quote, but I'll try, "When you know, they know, you know?" he quoted, nodding thoughtfully.

She smiled. For some reason, that non-sense sounded logical. "Yeah, I think maybe you and your friend are on to something. I will give it a try. Thank you, Tommy. I can't believe I'm saying this to you, but I feel much better about this."

Tommy smiled. "You're welcome."

"By the way, who said that to you?"

"It came straight from the turtle's mouth in *Nemo*...Dude Crush, something or other."

Katherine rolled her eyes and laughed. "Leave it to you to take advice from a kid's movie." She got out of the car and walked into the airport.

"You're welcome!" Tommy yelled. Katherine waved.

CHAPTER ELEVEN

Warren looked at his bedside clock; it was seven o'clock that night. He hadn't bothered to get out of bed since his date last night, not since the call that he received from Tommy this morning. He couldn't believe she just left without saying anything. What was the point? She made up her mind, and his for that matter. He didn't know what he did wrong to piss her off the night before.

He didn't think going back to his place to sleep with her would solve anything. Who knows maybe it would've? Women were different these days. He thought he provided her with a romantic date. Dinner, dancing, dress, jewelry, and shoes. *What the hell else could he have done?* Maybe he should have sung to her.

When Tommy called this morning, it was like the final missile blowing up his life. First his wife, and now Kat. He thought he loved Sarah more than anything. He never thought in a million years that there would be another woman in his life, but then Katherine came along. Whoever said "the greatest thing was to love and be loved in return," really had something. Never did he think he would be head over heels for someone and they just wouldn't really give a rat's ass.

He shook his head off his pillow and went to sit up just as the phone rang. Warren sighed as he looked down at the caller id. It was his sister, Sydney.

"Hey, sis," Warren sighed.

"Hey yourself, big brother. How's it going?"

"Well, it's been better. You?"

"Wanna talk about it?"

"Not really."

Then the doorbell rang.

"Hey, Syd, hold on a second. Someone's at the door. He placed the phone down on the dresser and took his pants off of the floor, pulling them over his boxers, and then grabbed a shirt out of his dresser. He picked back up the phone. "Syd, mind if I call you back later?"

"No, that's okay. I just wanted to let you know that I really liked Katherine. I thought she was funny, spirited... spunky."

"Yeah," Warren said closing his eyes. "That she is."

"Well, bye."

"Bye, sis."

He hung up the receiver as the doorbell chimed again. "Hold on a sec.," he said, then opened the door to none other than Tommy Jones. "Tommy?" Warren said, and then leaned in to see if anyone was with him.

"Yeah," Tommy replied, and then looked to his left then right. "What?"

"Nothing, this is a surprise."

"Really? Well, I just took Katherine to the airport."

"So you said."

"You do understand that she is gone, right?"

"What the hell, is this an intervention? Of course, I understand. It's what she wanted."

"Can I come in?" Tommy asked.

"Yeah, sorry. Want something to drink?"

"A beer would be fine. Have I ever told you about my good friend Dude?"

"No." Warren shook his head. "I don't think so."

"Well," Tommy began, "it happened about a month ago. She was drunk."

"Who was?"

"It really doesn't matter right now. All that matters is I don't love her anymore."

"The drunk?"

"No, the sister."

"Whose sister?"

"Karen's."

"You slept with Kat?" Warren yelled.

Tommy inhaled deeply and took a swig of beer. "Keep up, Doc, the other sister."

"You slept with Karen?"

"Technicalities, anyway,"

"Either you slept with her, or you didn't?"

"Are you going to listen to the story or not?"

"Alright, I'm listening."

"Well, you could listen a whole lot better with some wings and a pizza."

"Fine, we'll order in, let's go downstairs; continue."

"Alright, don't forget to ask for the blue cheese, they always bring ranch. I hate—"

"Tommy!"

"Fine, it's just that the ranch gives me the—"

"I will order the damn blue cheese! Now, if you please?"

"Okay, well, I was totally in love with this girl."

"Karen?"

"No, Katherine."

"I thought you said you didn't sleep with Kat?"

"Give me a break here, Doc. And you are the one that

went to medical school?"

"Fine," Warren huffed.

"I dated Kat, but I never slept with her. Anyway, I was in love with her for all these years. She has the greatest," Tommy gestured at his chest and curved his palms, before saying, "rack, you know?"

Without thinking, Warren smiled and nodded then slapped Tommy. "Jesus, man get on with the story."

"Ok, anyway, she was everything to me. I'm like her parent's favorite."

Somehow, Warren didn't believe that one, but he didn't feel an interruption would work.

"Anyway, so it would've been perfect; like one big happy family. Then this glorious night, I was at this great kegger at Ronnie Pilsted's place, and she was there, my angel in blue. She had a *Killians* in her hand and that dumbass with the goggles, you know, her latest, was sitting on the fence, beside her, talking and making her laugh. Well, the next thing I know, I'm up in the main house, and I have to piss something awful and she walks in on me in the bathroom and sees me doing my thing! Here the idiot said something stupid, so she ran into the bathroom to cry. It was like kismet! A meet cute... I had to piss, and she needed the bathroom! So, basically we fucked, and now I'm in love...."

Warren took his fingers from his hair and stared at the back of his hand. "How the hell does that have anything to do with me and my situation?"

Tommy just looked around in a smiling daze and then back to Warren. "I don't know, but it worked for Kat, so I thought that I would chance it, and get some free wings and beer out of you."

"Tommy, get the hell out of here, and leave Karen alone or I'm calling big Bill."

"You wouldn't!" he said as Warren ushered him out.

"I would." He shut the door. "What an idiot!" Warren laughed. "What a fucking idiot." He shook his head and turned the lock on the door. Why did he think he could get great advice from Tommy Jones? To think he said Katherine benefited from it? How in the hell did that make her happy; or help her even? Maybe she thought she would be better once she got to New York and tried someone else out? That's all he could really take from that stupid story. He didn't really care at this point. She made her choice, and now she was going to have to live with it.

CHAPTER TWELVE

First things first, Katherine thought as she walked into the small law office next to *High Fashion*. She smiled at the receptionist as she told them who she was and waited in the small sitting area. When the secretary told her she could go back, Katherine stood up, flattened her skirt down in the front and walked towards the back part of the law office. She met her lawyer halfway down the hall, hands extended in one big shake. "Congratulations, Katherine! We did it. *High Fashion* took the settlement, and might I say, well done. The recording that you got for us did the job. It was neck-and-neck there for a while, but that, baby, is how we do things!"

"Oh, thank God!"

***

Two months passed in a blur since she walked away from him. Warren worked in the clinic 24/7 it seemed, and he didn't leave any free time to spend with Bill or any of the others in the Daniels clan. The months were filled without fishing or talking, and definitely no *High Fashion Magazine*.

Bill could understand why. He knew how Warren felt about his Katherine. She was a special girl, but sometimes she needed a push in the right direction. And that's exactly what he was going to do, just a little push. There was absolutely no harm in that.

The door to the Free Clinic opened, letting in a gust of billowing snow. Dr. Vance sat at his desk, hands twined in his hair, looking down at something. When Bill's voice sounded, he stiffened.

"Evening, Doc., planning on spending the night?"

"Bill. No, sir. Just finishing up on a case," he said as he slid what he was looking at under a few sheets of paper. Bill recognized it as he watched him push it aside. His wife had taken a picture of Warren and Kat. She gave it to him a few days before Kat left.

"You know, Warren. She's miserable, too."

Warren looked up with tired eyes. "Who's miserable?"

"Warren, don't play dumb with me. You know exactly *who* I'm talking about," Bill said as he took a chair right in front of Warren.

"Well, then she knows what to do. She knows where I am, Bill. She knows where I live, and she knows my number. For Christ sake, Bill, she knows where you are."

"Warren Vance, don't you use the Lord's name in vain. I know she *knows* all of that. You know how *she* is... stubborn. I don't know where she gets it, probably her mother." Bill's eyes twinkled, as Warren scoffed.

"Well, I don't feel like getting hurt anymore, Bill. If she wants me, then she knows what to do. I'm getting along perfectly fine here."

Now it was Bill's turn to scoff, "Yeah, Doc, it looks like it. Is that a twenty-four hour shadow growing on your face? Your bags under your eyes look just like Tommy's dog, Tobias. Not to mention, boy, you look downright awful. I haven't seen you in a while. You used to come out and see me. No more fishing..." Bill shook his head from left to right, really laying it on thick.

"Thanks for the lecture, old man..."

"Old man? Now you see here—"

"You're old, Bill. And I, for your information, am trying

to grow a beard."

"It looks like the beard is growing you," Bill joked.

"Very funny, and *fishing*? It's freezing out there. Damn near Christmas. So, I would have thought you would have understood."

"Well, *Warren,* I would have understood if it were a day or two, maybe even a week, but a few months? I know how you feel about Katherine. You like her, right?"

Warren shuffled his feet, and got up to go to the water dispenser. He grabbed a cup, and then filled it slowly.

"Warren, answer me, God damn it!"

Warren's eyes widened. "Don't use the Lord's name in vain, Bill!"

"I'll do as I damn well please, I'm allowed to. Remember, I'm old. Besides, I think I have the right to know, she's my daughter!" Bill yelled, waiting for Warren's answer.

"I love her, alright? I just don't have it in me to go traipsing all over New York if she doesn't feel the same for me. I've already been through hell with Sarah, but this... this is killing me. She is kill—"

Bill walked over to him and put his hands on Warren's shoulders. "Then you know what to do; go to her. She's at her place in New York. Gail wrote down the address for you on this card; she sends her best. You better go soon though, son. The last time I talked to her, she didn't sound very good."

Warren swallowed. "What's wrong with her?"

"I don't know, you're the Doc, why don't you go check it out?

"Is this another ploy, Bill?"

Bill just smiled and handed him the card with the address and started for the door. "It may be..." He winked at him and grinned. "But don't you want to find out?"

Bill walked out the door, leaving Warren standing there, card in hand, and mouth open. Warren wondered if this was all just a big scam to get him to go see her. He was sure that it was, but if it wasn't, he would have to find out if Katherine was alright. He picked up his bag and pulled his coat over his shoulders as he heard the door open once again.

"We're closed," he said as he looked up, noticing Bill Daniels standing in the door once again.

"Oh, and Warren...there's always ice fishing! So, get your head out of your ass, bring my kitten home, and come over next Friday for some fishing. The missus is going to bake, and we all know how good she is at that."

Warren just smiled as Bill shut the door once more. He missed that old coot. He just hoped he was telling the truth about Katherine. He hoped that she was miserable without him, too.

***

She awoke that morning to a pounding headache and nausea that could knock out a three hundred pound man. Clutching the toilet, she threw up the last of her salad from the night before and the three Tylenol that she took moments before. "What a waste that was," she said disgustedly. She took the towel off the rack and wiped her forehead and her mouth. When she heard the door buzzer, she felt like she was going to die. "Oh, God," she said as she stood up and went to the intercom. "Yes?"

"Katherine?" the voice called out.

Oh, my God! She hadn't heard that voice in a while. She pushed the button on the buzzer to let him up, and then ran back to the bathroom, brushed her teeth, threw up once more only to hear a knock on the door. Using mouthwash this time, she gurgled then spit.

"Be right there!" She went to her bedroom, put her best blouse on, and pulled her jeans up. Going for the buttons, she gasped, too tight. "Damn!" She grabbed another pair of jeans out of the closet—same problem. "What the fuck!" she yelled. "Hold on, sorry, hold on!"

She decided that she must have shrunk everything at that cheap ass laundry matt on the corner of State and Main. She grabbed her robe, pulled it tight, fixed her hair with her hand, and then went to the door. She opened it to reveal Warren, looking great, and much like he did in her dreams.

"Hi," she whispered softly, panting a little from her clothing stint.

"Hi, you look good, a little flushed...are you okay?" He looked concerned. A little different, still handsome as ever, a *little thinner* she thought. At least one of them was looking out for number one.

"No, I'm okay. I just woke up. I've been tired lately. I'm not used to sleeping this long, plus I've been sick."

"Oh, sorry, would you like me to give you a check-up? Eat anything weird lately? Maybe some bad Chinese?"

Small talk, she should invite him in. "No Chinese. Weird food? Yes, a little, but I eat weird things all of the time. Want to come in?"

"Yeah, I was hoping to." He flushed slightly as he walked in, noticing some of her laundry on the door. He turned to look around; the place was very small, considering where she came from. "Nice place."

"Thanks, I like it." *That's a lie.* "I, Warren, when did you get in? Why didn't you tell me you were coming?"

Warren looked down at his feet and put his hands in his pockets. "Sorry, I had a medical conference and thought I would come see you. You're the only person I know here in New York."

"Oh, work. Sorry, I misunderstood. It's great seeing you again! What's it been now, two months?" *Two months, fourteen days, eight hours and thirty-nine, no forty-minutes...to be exact.*

"Yeah, a little longer give or take a few days." He smiled, taking in the rest of the place, afraid to look at her eyes. She looked good. She finally gained a few pounds, much too skinny the last time. Her face seemed flush, and she looked like she was going to be nauseous.

"I..." She stood up. "Excuse me." She ran into the bathroom, barely making it to the toilet, and then she threw up once more.

Warren stood up, ran into the bathroom and pulled her hair back. She turned for the towel and he already had it under the sink, warming it. He wiped off her forehead and mouth. She stood up.

"Thank you, oh, God, I feel awful. There must be a virus going around. I've felt like this for a few weeks, but this is the first time I've ever puked. I'm so embarrassed. I certainly didn't picture our next meeting with you holding my hair." She had to laugh at that one.

"Maybe you should go to the hospital, get some blood work done. If it's a virus, there's nothing much they can do, but they can make you comfortable at least."

He was concerned for her, and she felt numb. For the past two months she had wanted to fly home and tell him how she felt. She wanted to kiss him so badly right now, but it didn't seem right to infect him with whatever she had. "I don't know. I really don't like—"

"Just like your father, stubborn," he said, a little irritated.

"I'm not... Yes, maybe a little. If you think I should, I will, but I will warn you, I'm a little slow. I haven't been walking that much lately. I haven't been leaving the house."

"Why? Is something wrong? Have you been fired?" He looked into her eyes and waited for the truth.

"Yes and no."

"What kind of answer is that? Yes, you got fired, or no you didn't?"

"Yes, something is wrong, I haven't been able to keep food down yet, never mind, you won't understand. And, no, I didn't get fired. I quit my job."

"You quit your job?"

"Yes, I—"

"I promise we will talk later." Warren shook his head. "You look pale, we really should get you to the hospital."

"Don't you have your conference? I don't want you to have to miss anything."

"Katherine, there, listen, I'm taking you to the hospital whether you like it or not, now get your purse, and your insurance card, we're leaving."

"I have to get dressed," she said, and then started to break down in tears. "Oh, God," she cried.

"What? What's wrong?"

"My pants don't fit! I shrunk them all, all of them!" she cried hysterically. "I don't have anything—"

"It's okay, calm down. Do you have a sundress or something like that?"

She started sniffling; it was cute. He didn't have the heart to tell her that it looked like she put on a few pounds; he thought she looked better.

"Yes, I have a dress, I'll be back." She turned around and grabbed a dress out of her closet, and then went into her bathroom and changed. "I don't understand! This is tight, this has never been! I'm such a mess."

"You're not a mess, you look good, and who cares if you put on a few pounds. I think you look wonderful."

Kat came out. He smiled, and she wasn't.

"A FEW POUNDS?" she snarled. "I haven't gained any weight! I..."

"I'm sorry, Katherine, It's okay, I just—let's go to the hospital, you look perfect. Please, stop crying." He really was making a mess out of this. "Here," he said, grabbing her arm, and leading her out the door.

They crawled into the back of a Taxi a few minutes later. Katherine felt too sick to tease Warren about how awkward he looked hailing a cab. It took him seven tries. He had his arm around her in the back seat. The close proximity between them made her shiver just thinking about him. She wondered if he still loved her. She didn't think a second of the day went by without her thinking of him. She could almost taste his lips.

"How's your practice doing?" she asked, trying to keep to small talk.

"Good. I have a few new patients. I'm ready to move into a bigger office. How's...never mind."

"What?"

"Well, it's just that you couldn't stay in Connecticut because of your job, at least that's what I thought." The traffic was awful; the taxi lurched and stopped and lurched and stopped. Katherine kept making gagging noises. It would take a few more minutes before they made it to the hospital that was less than a half block from her apartment. Thank God he didn't live here.

"Well, I...I had a hard time when I came back; I'm surprised Mom and Dad didn't tell you. I couldn't keep up living here without... Well, like I said, I quit my job. I applied for a job with The New York Times, and I didn't get it. Turns out the woman that was going to retire decided not to. You obviously haven't read *High Fashion* for a while?"

"No, I found it hard to do after you left. As for your parents, I haven't seen them either. I can't bring myself to see them. You look too much like your mother, and you have your father's spirit in you. He's been in the office a few times, but it's not like it used to be."

Kat frowned. She had no idea how bad it had gotten for him.

They pulled into the hospital parking lot; she barely made it out the Taxi before she threw up once more. The cabby turned his nose away and scrunched his face. "That'll be eighteen fifty." Warren shook his head, shocked at the price of a half block ride. He fished out a twenty quickly then rushed to Katherine's side. "Keep the change," he called to the driver. The Taxi rushed off.

Warren steadied Katherine as she finished heaving "You wouldn't think there would be anything left in there Let me help you." She looked run down, and most certainly didn't look like she'd been taking care of herself either.

"You don't have to help me anymore, Warren. I can manage."

"Don't be ridiculous, I'm going in there with you."

"Why? I've made your life hell? Why'd you even come and see me?"

"I'm worried about you, Kat. You look like hell."

"It's not your responsibility. I'm not," she said as she started walking towards the door. She felt an odd sensation in her stomach, and put her hand on it. "Woo," she said, "that was weird.

"What?"

"I don't know, just a flutter."

"Come on, you are worrying me by the minute. Let's go."

After two hours of waiting in the lobby, Kat finally got into the curtained area. Warren insisted on coming back with her, not having the energy to deal with it, she didn't argue. They took her blood, and gave her a physical.

"The doctor will be in to see you in a few more minutes, Mrs. Daniels," the nurse said as she smiled and bowed out.

"Miss," Katherine muttered. "Why do they always assume that you're married?"

"Well, you're with me in here. What does it matter what they think?" Warren spouted off. "Do you want me to leave when the doctor gets in here?"

"No, what's the point, they're not going to do anything. I've asked for pain meds for the past two hours and all I get is *smiles*. What is that? It's so damn hot in here!"

"Hot? It's not hot in here. I feel like buying a sweatshirt from the gift shop. What the hell, Katherine? Where did you say you...?"

A dark-complexioned man walked in with his clipboard, his name on the tab said Williamson. "Mr. and Mrs. Daniels, I'm Dr. Williamson." He smiled broadly. Kat rolled her eyes at the mention of her last name and looked at Warren. "I really don't see any problems here at all. Everything looks good. I would say about eleven weeks."

"What are you talking about? I feel awful." Kat looked up, terrified. "Wait, what? I only have eleven weeks, to what, live?"

The doctor looked at her surprisingly. "Mrs. Daniels, I thought you must have known? You're pregnant, nearing the end of your first trimester. Everything looks terrific, but you will want to schedule yourself an appointment with an OB soon. We like to keep track of everything during pregnancy. Congratulations! I will send the nurse back in with the discharge papers and a list of OBGYNs." He waved goodbye at the two.

Katherine's face was frozen in shock. Warren's was spread out in a huge grin. "We're pregnant!" he exclaimed.

"I—I guess so, oh my God. Oh, my God" she started crying. Her hands went up to her face and started bawling.

"Katherine, are you okay?"

"Yes, I'm okay, I'm great. Here I thought I was just getting fat and losing my mind!" She laughed then wiped her eyes, "I'm so..."

"I love you so much, there wasn't a conference. I came here hoping to bring you home with me. Please, come home with me."

"I love you, too! I—I lied earlier. I've been miserable, sick and throwing up for the past few weeks, gaining weight, eating Rocky-Road like it's going to expire, and I quit my job at *High Fashion* before I even went to Connecticut! I was just too embarrassed about it. Besides, I thought for sure that I had the job at the Times."

He brought his arms around her and held her tight. "Katherine, I'm so happy, I love you so much." He dropped down to one knee and pulled out a box from his coat pocket. "Marry me, Katherine?"

Kat cried as she nodded. She waited for him to stand up, and then she wrapped her arms around his neck and pressed her lips against his. "Yes, yes," she said.

"Yes?" Warren pulled back, smiling.

"Yes, definitely, yes! I love you so much. I now know that I can't survive without you!"

"I can't survive without you either! Everything has been so miserable for me without you. I'll live wherever you want. I'll get a job here if that's what it takes, but I will never let you out of my reach again."

"Oh, Warren," she cried. "I want to go home with you. I should've known from the beginning that we were meant to be. I think I was the only fool that didn't."

"We are pretty perfect together, aren't we?" He smiled broadly. "I love you."

"I love you, too."

THREE DAYS LATER

"**I** just hope she apologizes," Karen said, looking over to Tommy in the Airport lobby.

"Aw, come on. You really don't think hard-headed Kat is going to apologize, do you? She still owes *me* one."

Karen looked annoyed. "For what?" She'd known Tommy was obsessed with her older sister, but thought that was pretty much over.

"Now, Karen," Tommy crooned, smiling. "I think you may be a little jealous." Karen's face turned red. "She owes me an apology for turning your old man against me. I never did anything to deserve that. I swear, sometimes he looks at me like he wants to ring my neck. It's almost like he thought your sister and I slept together."

Karen turned her head fast and looked right into Tommy's eyes. "You mean to tell me you didn't?" Karen asked, shocked. She took a deep breath as he stared at her.

"Of course not, Kar. I don't think I could've even if I had the chance to. She's more like a sister to me," he said, walking closer to Karen. He put his arms around her waist, and leaned in to whisper softly, "Now, you on the other hand, I can't keep my hands off of."

Karen took a deep breath and stepped out of his embrace just as the loud speaker sounded.

"Flight 211 from New York has arrived safely, with a time of one hour and ten minutes."

"That's them," Karen said. She was red-faced from what Tommy said. "I..."

"Karen," Katherine said softly as she walked towards

her from the tunnel. "I'm so, so sorry! You were so right, and I—how can I not even know what I want?"

"You've got to be *freaking* kidding me," Tommy said.

"Ignore him." Karen laughed. "I'm sorry, too! I missed you so much, and I'm so glad that you finally got your head out of your ass!"

"Nice one, Karen." Kat laughed; Warren chuckled, too, as he put his arm around her.

They looked so happy; so incredible together.

"We have some news to tell you," Kat said as she looked from her sister and Tommy to Warren.

"Well, I guessed that much. We, Tommy and I thought you were going to say you were getting married! Congrats!" Karen said happily, as they walked through the airport to the baggage claim.

"No, even better." Warren smiled.

"What could be better than that?" Tommy asked, surprising everyone. "I thought that's what you were going to do when you got to New York?"

"No, we *are* getting married, but that's not what Kat's talking about."

Karen and Tommy exchanged glances, looking confused. Karen sighed, "What?"

"We're pregnant!" Katherine squealed. Her face broke out in an irresistible grin. Karen's eyes widened and Tommy smiled.

"Oh, congratulations!" Tommy said, shaking Warren's hand and hugging Katherine. "This is wonderful news! Bill's going to flip!"

"You're going to be a mommy?" Karen cried. "Oh my God, you're going to be a mommy!"

"It's wonderful, isn't it? A mommy! I never thought I would. We only just found out, and of course, we couldn't be any happier," Katherine said as she grabbed hold of Warren's hand. He smiled at her lovingly.

Karen felt a stabbing at her chest. Her sister was really happy, and she was happy, too, but jealous at the same time.

An hour later, they were all celebrating at Morton's steak house in downtown, Connecticut. Tommy, Karen, Gail, Bill, and Warren and Kat had more laughs that night than Kat thought she had ever had in her whole life.

It was funny how you think your life is over one minute, and the next it feels like it's just beginning. That's how was with Warren; a whirlwind of new experiences, falling in love, becoming a mother, and now getting married to her soul mate, her Warren. Somehow, it felt surreal, and on the other hand it felt like it happened before.

***

God looked down at the family and friends celebrating life and love. He turned to the newest angel to come home. Sarah's eyes were wet as He suspected.

"We did it," she said, looking to God. "We did it!"

God smiled, and put His arm around her shoulders. His warmth spread throughout her body. She felt happy and complete for the first time in her whole life. She finally did something for someone, unselfishly and unconditionally; she felt whole.

"I'm proud of you, Sarah. I'm proud of Katherine. She did a good job with her last chance. She did us proud."

"Yes, she did, and to think they're going to have a baby," Sarah cried. "I'm so happy that she could give Warren that. He's going to be a wonderful father."

"And she will be a great mother."

"What about the other couple sitting with her? What do you think will happen with them?" Sarah asked as she glanced down at Tommy and Karen. They were sitting next to each other laughing over a shared basket of onion rings.

"Ah, funny you should say that. It's here in the book," God said as He pointed to a large book on a golden pedestal. The cover was titled "The Book of Life" in golden letters. He opened it and thumbed through the pages until He stumbled on a picture of the two younger people at the table.

"Right here they are," God said. "Thomas Jones and Karen Daniels." He shook his head. "They're going to be a harder sell, but they are definitely what you down below call 'soul mates'."

"Really?" Sarah sighed. "I would like to help."

"Good. We've just got to give them a little push."

"I'll be happy to," Sarah said, smiling. She took one last look at Warren and Katherine and grinned.

God followed her gaze, and then cleared His throat. "Let's leave them to their planning, shall we?" God took her arm and lead her to a golden staircase. "It's your job to get the two of them to realize that they love each other. Do you think you can do that?" God looked down at Karen and Tommy and then back to Sarah.

"I know I can," she said as she descended the staircase into the living. "I know I can."

EPILOGUE

As the wedding party walked into the large reception hall, Bill Daniels began taking pictures of his eldest daughter. She smiled and posed for him several times, as her husband held onto her hand, gliding her from here to there. Gail and Bill danced on more than one occasion, and when it was time for the speeches, Bill stood up and raised his glass. "To my beautiful daughter, and my new son-in-law, he's a doctor by the way," Bill said, as he moved his shoulders up and down. People laughed as he continued, "As I was saying, these two kids were meant for each other, and that's why we're here today. We're not only celebrating them, but we are celebrating the fact that we only have one kid left at home. Isn't that right, Karen!" Bill cheered. People all around started laughing, and Karen rolled her eyes, held up her champagne flute, and nodded a toast. As she threw the drink back, Bill laughed heartily. "Anyway, six down one to go, Mazletoff!" People at the wedding looked curiously as some shouted back and cheered; most just drank the contents down and started talking again.

***

As Warren slipped off her garter, catcalls were heard from all around. All the single men and some of the little kids that were running around moments before all waited for him to toss it; the tradition being, of course, whomever caught the garter and the bridal bouquet would be in for a fate worse than death, as Tommy Jones had put it minutes before. However graceful his words were, he still offered to remove the garter from Kat's leg. Even for Tommy, that

198

was going a little too far.

Katherine smiled at the group as she recovered from Warren's hand being so far up on her thigh. Warren twirled the garter on his finger and Katherine lowered her bouquet as they turned their backs and waited for the queue from the DJ. They both tossed them out. She tossed hers over her head and Warren used the garter like a slingshot, propelling it into the crowd. As hands groped and people looked, the two that caught them couldn't have been more taken by surprise.

Tommy caught the garter atop his head, and the flowers landed right on Karen's lap—she wasn't even trying to catch them.

As their eyes met, nothing was heard, and then out of nowhere the familiar voice of Bill Daniels called out, "Oh, hell no!"

The Art of Seduction
Book II
Thomas & Karen

The Party

The party was in full swing as Ronnie Pilsted made his way from the kitchen into the living room. Beer bottles and plastic cups littered the table as he worked his way around the room with a trashcan. There were people there that he'd never seen in his life, and the music was so loud that one could definitely lose their hearing. When he saw his best bud, Tommy, walk in, he clasped his hands together tightly.

"Tommy, I didn't think you were coming. You wanna shot?"

"God yes; school was a real bitch tonight."

"What, you crack a nail, man?"

"Very funny, no. There's just a bunch of slackers in my new class. I had to explain the pottery wheel for a half an hour longer than it should've taken."

"That sucks. Hey, can you believe we're sitting here talking about a pottery wheel on a Friday night, when there are a whole bunch of lovely ladies out there with barely any clothes on? We *are* getting old," Ronnie said, laughing as he gestured with his bottle of *Coors* to the door.

Tommy shook his head and snorted. "Fuck, I haven't thought of another girl since high school, and you know the one I'm talking about. Women are trouble; I'd rather talk shop any day of the week."

"Yeah, I guess you're right. Whoa, hey," Ronnie said, gesturing with his beer once more, but this time to the doorway. "Isn't that your flame's baby sis?"

Tommy turned around and saw Karen walking in with her boyfriend, Joe. Her father dubbed the boyfriend *goggle-man*. "Yeah that's her and her boyfriend, Joe."

"Shit, she's all grown up!" Ronnie smiled over his bottle as he brought it up to his lips for a drink. "Look at them legs!"

Tommy looked at those legs many times before now, but when Ronnie mentioned them, he grew a little mad at the remark. It must've been because she was like a sister to him, he thought. Nevertheless, when he looked at her hanging on the arm of that goofy Joe Watkins, something bubbled up inside of him that made him go straight for Ronnie's refrigerator and grab a beer.

"Women," Ronnie said.

"Yeah." Tommy shook his head.

A half-hour into the party, Tommy found himself glancing more than once over to Karen and her boyfriend. Joe was rather boisterous with his arm movements and stories. At one point of the evening, he heard Joe talking about his music class and how he was auditioning for the *Tonight Show Band*. This guy was so full of shit that he stunk half way across the room. He saw Karen make many attempts to change the conversation, but he kept everything about himself and her as his piece of eye candy.

She had her amused face on right now as they made

eye contact. It was the first time that evening that she even noticed he was there. She smiled, and something in his chest constricted. It must've had something to do with a private joke of theirs. He didn't know.

She made many different faces that night. The thin line of a smile that she used while she tried to look interested was his favorite. He caught himself looking over at her many times just to see which one she wore.

She playfully looked back when Joe started talking about his guitar as if it were a lover or a family member. She rolled her eyes and blew air up at her bangs, and Tommy found himself laughing and grabbing another beer. After about three hours of watching and listening, he made his way over to her just as another woman walked into the party, his ex-girlfriend, Layla Winters.

"Tommy Jones, I didn't know you would be here," Layla drawled as she walked toward him.

Yes she did. Why wouldn't he? He'd been friends with Ronnie since the fifth grade. He could almost hear the wheels turning in the ditz's brain. She never was the smartest girl.

At first, when he met Layla, he thought she was smart. *No*, scratch that. She had a nice ass. And as far as nice asses were concerned, they went a long way when you were in the ninth grade and you were looking to get a piece of one.

"Hey, Layla," Tommy said as he brought the beer to his lips.

"Still in school?" Layla asked. She tossed her hair over her shoulder.

"Still in school. Still doing makeup at the mall?"

Layla smiled as if he were the only one in the room, and then brought her bottom lip under her teeth. "Yes, I just love doing makeup. It's so *glamorous*..."

God, he should have known better than to bring it up; she continued to speak and bored him of her aspirations of doing makeup for her hero, *the Goddess,* as she put it, Angelina Jolie. He would have to pretend to be interested. He would nod when she got exasperated, and smile at other times. Karen looked over at him, and they shared a smile. Layla was too busy in her talks about makeup to notice. Karen brought her eyebrows up in an arch and laughed.

She must have remembered Layla from high school. *Who didn't?* Everyone knew Layla Winters' name. Well, at least half of the drama club and football team did; really any male member of society would remember that ass and those white gym shorts. Karen moved closer as if she were going to come save him from his hell!

He smiled.

Layla seemed pleased with herself. She shook her head a few times letting her hair move around her face. The action reminded him of one of those hair actors that did a move like that before they had a psychotic episode. Karen brushed his arm as she went in for another beer, and just the touch of her arm against his skin brought him from his trance. *What the hell?*

"And that's when I knew I would meet her!" Layla said.

"Meet who?" Tommy asked, shaking his head. His mind was on Karen again.

"Angelina. Duh, Tommy, let's get out of here!" she said, batting her eyelashes and licking her lips for effect.

Tommy shook his head. "I can't, Layla. It sounds like a nice offer, but—" He noticed his buddy Ronnie by the refrigerator and motioned him over. Layla looked confused, but hopeful.

"Ronnie, Layla wants to be a makeup artist for the stars. Layla, Ronnie has three bedrooms upstairs and owns property in Bel Air."

Layla turned from Tommy to Ronnie so fast that a doctor might have to be called for whiplash, and smiled. Tommy bolted for the steps.

"Crazy bitch," Tommy mumbled, taking a few steps at a time and ran straight for the bathroom door.

***

Karen hadn't seen Ronnie Pilsted since high school. She only knew him because of his baby sister, Rachel. Rachel was in the band and did Yearbook at Hartford High. She was also the cheerleading captain.

She'd heard of the party when she went into Wilsons to get her watch fixed. The older man that worked at the counter took the day off, and his grandson, Grayson Bradley mentioned it. He even handed out fliers. She never intended on going. It's not like she was a lame person, or someone that didn't like to have fun; she just never felt comfortable in the party scene. She didn't even like going to bars. They made her feel uncomfortable. But when her boyfriend saw the flier sticking out of her jean's pocket, he grabbed it and instantly made the decision of going to the party.

"Come on, Karen, it's the perfect opportunity for me to hand out business cards, you know—some promotion for my band."

"I don't know, Joe. I went to high school with some of these people; I don't feel comfortable handing out fliers advertising you. It's just, I don't know. I don't like it.

"Karen, you know we're going," Joe said as if it were already a done deal. "Besides, it's a party, and where there's a party, there's free booze!"

Karen rolled her eyes. She was getting quite tired of following Joe around like some sick puppy. She'd been doing it way too much lately. At first, the attraction was somewhat rebellious. Her parents hated Joe. His *goggles*... they would call them, and it really irritated the piss out of her father. Her mother didn't like the way he fondled Karen either. Actually, she didn't like it herself, but she got used to it. Things like romance didn't really happen to her. She never had anything romantic ever happen to her. She was used to eating hotdogs and Ramen noodles with her boyfriends.

When they walked into the party, Joe immediately started for the tub with the beers in it. He grabbed two and pulled a small keychain out of his pocket with a bottle opener on it. *Talk about lush.* It was too embarrassing to be with him. This was definitely the last straw.

"Karen Daniels!" Rachel called from the steps as if they were best friends. Rachel ran and threw her arms around Karen. Rachel's hips grew at least two sizes since Karen saw her last, and she had a weird mole on her nose that had a tiny hair growing out of it. "I'm so glad that you came!"

"Rachel," Karen said as Joe tipped his beer to the woman, "how have you been?"

"Oh god, we have so much to talk about. Do you remember Walter Stanley?"

Walter Stanley. Yes, she remembered him. Captain of the Chess Club, and he wrote for the school newspaper. Rachel used to make fun of Walter on a daily basis.

"Yes, is he here?" Karen looked around the room.

"Oh, well I have some news!"

Karen *couldn't* wait. She turned back toward Rachel. "News?"

"Look," Rachel said, as she held her hand in front of Karen; the biggest diamond that Karen had ever seen dazzled proudly from Rachel's ring finger. "He just asked me!"

"Wow!" E*ven this bitch with a hairy mole got engaged. Just depressing*. "That is..."

"Great, I know. I should have known back in high school; he was so..."

Dorky was the only word that came to Karen's mind, but as far as she was concerned, he was more of a catch than Rachel was. "That's wonderful, Rachel! Congratulations!"

Joe cleared his throat, bringing the attention back to himself. Karen and Rachel looked.

"Hi, I'm Joe Watkins, Karen's significant other."

"Oh?" Rachel smiled giddily. "You're married!"

"No," Karen said abruptly, changing her stance with Joe. "We're not..."

"Well actually I'm in a band called *Future Reality*. I'm the lead singer, and I also play electric guitar."

"Oh," Rachel said confused. "That's nice." She turned and looked at Karen with the "I feel so sorry for you look."

206

"Yes, if you need someone to play for your wedding, here's my card," Joe said, handing a black card with a space ship on the front and reality stamped in red overtop.

"Oh, this is nice," Rachel said slowly.

"Joe," Karen said shortly.

Joe put his arm around Karen. She slugged it off. Rachel grimaced and mouthed sorry to Karen before she walked away.

"What the hell was that?"

"What, baby?"

"Why did you tell her you were my *significant other*? And why on God's earth did you offer to play for *her* wedding?"

"Well, I had to tell her something. We all know that you are *never* getting married, and I needed some gigs— just playing on the romantic side for some cash that's all."

"What!? Why would you say that *I'm* never getting married?"

"Well, don't take this the wrong way, but you're sort of frigid, and this," he said as he gestured to himself, and then to her chest, "was all just about the sex."

"Well, if that's the truth, then I've been seriously lacking in that department!"

"I didn't want to say anything..."

"What do you mean by *that*? So, you're saying that *I* wasn't any good?" Karen yelled. People at the party started to look at her. She looked around and noticed that Tommy was now gone, and Ronnie Pilsted was in a deep conversation with Layla Winters. Rachel sat on the couch gossiping with her newest victim, Carrie Johnson—another girl she didn't give the time of day to in high school.

"Well, yeah."

Karen's eyes rounded. She took what was left of her beer and turned it over on his head. It ran down his face as he yelled, "Crazy bitch!" She turned around and ran straight for the steps. The bathroom seemed like a great place to hide.

***

Tommy stood in front of Ronnie's porcelain throne, and tried to aim. The beer started to get to him. It wasn't as if he didn't drink, it's just that he'd never tried to down an entire liquor store all in one night. The target that he aimed for was a hard-water stain in the middle, and he was having a hard time at that. As he gently tucked himself away and zipped up his pants, the door flung open, and a short intake of breath stopped him in his stance.

Then he heard *her* crying.

Karen.

He turned to find her standing there; her eyes were drenched with tears, and her hands went to her mouth.

"Oh my god!" she yelped. "I'm so sorry, I'm—" She just stood there staring at him.

"I'm—let me wash my hands," is all he could say. He turned around, pumped some *Purel* into his palm, and rubbed his hands together. "Karen, are you okay? What happened?"

"I," she choked. "I'm so sorry! I'm making a huge mess of things tonight."

"What are you talking about?" Tommy asked as he moved closer to her. He stumbled. He felt more than light-headed, the closer he got. His finger lightly traced a newly formed tear that made its way down to her chin. She swallowed. She looked up at him and something inside of him changed.

He had to kiss her.

Just then, a rush of emotions took over him, and he grabbed her tightly in his arms and placed his mouth of hers. Her own arms wrapped around his neck and brought him into her, and they stumbled backwards, straight into the shower curtain and fell back into the wall. Hands grabbed and tore at clothes, lips bit, kisses were planted, his breathing accelerated...

He woke up first, noting the added weight to his chest. He opened his eyes. He wasn't dreaming. Karen was draped over him, one curl splayed against her forehead, and the rest of her hair spilled over onto his chest. He took a deep breath; she smelled so good.

At some point, he could vaguely remember showering with her. He looked up and saw the sun shining through the blinds. They were still at Ronnie's house, and he only had one bathroom. Then he heard the rapping on the door. Karen jolted. He put his palm over her mouth, and her eyes widened. "Shh..."

"Hey, whoever the hell you are, I need to piss; so hurry up and get your business done!" Ronnie yelled from the outside.

Karen looked up into Tommy's eyes. Tommy slowly removed his palm, and he held up one finger. "Ronnie, sorry, it's going to be a few minutes. I drank way too much last night, and I've been sick." Tommy looked down at Karen; she went to move, but he held her firmly in his grip.

"Oh shit, man, that's okay. I'll go find some woods outside. Take your time."

"Thanks, man."

"Oh my god," Karen whispered. She started to panic as she covered herself with a towel from the rack. "Oh, my,"

"God," Tommy finished for her. He couldn't help but watch her as she dressed. He knew it was the perverse thing to do, but somehow he didn't care.

"What did we do?" she asked, and then flushed as she shook her head not believing it herself.

"What *didn't* we do?" Tommy retorted. He grinned as she looked back at him. She took a bar of soap and aimed it right for him. He still sat in the tub with nothing on but a morning erection.

"Cover yourself up, why don't you!" Karen yelled.

Tommy laughed. "Karen, I think it's a little late for subtleties."

"Tommy, I don't even know what to...."

"You don't have to say anything. Last night was..."

"Don't say anything." Karen looked positively horrified.

"Don't say a mistake, Karen, because from what I remember, and I remember *a lot*, it was great."

Karen's face redden and smiled sheepishly. "I have to find a way of getting out of here, unnoticed. Oh, *fuck*!"

Tommy laughed again, stood up and grabbed his boxers and jeans from the floor. "What?"

"I don't have a ride, and I'm pretty sure Joe isn't here anymore."

"*Joe?* Oh Jesus, Karen. You have a boyfriend!"

"Not anymore."

Just that little admission made his heart jump. "What

do you mean?"

"That's why I came in here; we broke up."

"So, I'm the rebound?" he asked. She stiffened, but he smiled. "I don't really give a shit *how* it happened, Karen. I'm just glad it did."

"Tommy!"

"What?"

"Can you just shut up for a minute? I need to think." Karen went to the window and peered down, trying to see if she saw any people hanging around. The only thing she saw was Ronnie peeing in the bushes. She rolled her eyes.

"What?" Tommy asked, laughing.

"Ronnie, he's...uh."

Tommy grinned when he saw what she was looking at. "I'll take you home, and it's not that high from here," he said, pulling the blinds from the window. "There's some lattice on the side of the house. Wait for me, and I'll go outside and catch you."

"You're insane," Karen said, and then smiled up at Tommy.

Tommy grabbed his shoes and kissed her forehead. "I'll see you in a few minutes."

Read this and other great stories from
Firefly & Wisp Books!
Check out our website at www.fireflyandwispbooks.com
for details!

You can order your copy of The Art of Seduction today!

Click the link below to be redirected to

The Art of Seduction's Amazon Page.

Danielle Lee Zwissler is an Ohio author. She is a big fan of romance as well as fantasy. She likes her characters to have larger than life personalities, a fair amount of money, and if possible, red hair!

The first book that she had published was "Her Last Chance" and immediately after was the second book of the Daniels Dynasty,"The Art of Seduction". Soon after, Books-to-go-Now! put out an erotic title of hers "The Trio of Sin".

Now, Danielle is currently working with four different publishers as well as a group of writers called "The Iron Writer Challenge" a challenge in which 5 writers compete against one another with stories that they've written of only 500 words! Thus far, Danielle has won 8 out of the 11 challenges that she has taken.

Currently her list of novels includes several erotica, written under the pen name Heather Lane, western romance, romantic comedies, flash fiction, and soon to be released a young adult fantasy series!

Danielle believes her storytelling and love of writing stems from reading J.K. Rowling's Harry Potter Series as well as great romance writers, Linda Lael Miller, Bella Andre, and Diana Palmer.

If you are in the Ohio area, and would like to visit with Danielle, you can most likely find her at a book convention, or hanging out at the local library. Or you can contact her through her email at: authordanielleleezwissler@gmail.com, her website-www.danielleleezwissler.com, twitter-twitter.com/danielleleezwis, or on facebook @ www.facebook.com/danielleleezwissle

Made in the USA
Middletown, DE
24 July 2016